Backyard Horse
Tales

Backyard Horse Tales

SOX

Jackie Anton

Copyright © 2011 by Jackie Anton.

Library of Congress Control Number: 2010919388
ISBN: Hardcover 978-1-4568-4301-4
Softcover 978-1-4568-4300-7
Ebook 978-1-4568-4302-1

All rights reserved. No part of this book may be reproduced or transmitted in any form or by any means, electronic or mechanical, including photocopying, recording, or by any information storage and retrieval system, without permission in writing from the copyright owner.

This is a work of fiction. Names, characters, places and incidents either are the product of the author's imagination or are used fictitiously, and any resemblance to any actual persons, living or dead, events, or locales is entirely coincidental.

This book was printed in the United States of America.

To order additional copies of this book, contact:
Xlibris Corporation
1-888-795-4274
www.Xlibris.com
Orders@Xlibris.com

CONTENTS

1. A New World 1
2. Small Town U.S.A. 11
3. Learning the Ropes 17
4. Shot Down by Gunner 31
5. New Horizons 45
6. Just Say Whoa! 49
7. Icing the Cake 67
8. The Storm 75
9. Back in the Game 89
10. Stepping into a New Role 99

Appendix 105

This book is dedicated all those who have ever loved a special horse and for Sox's many fans.

ACKNOWLEDGMENTS

A special thank you to my daughter, Patricia, for brainstorming sessions and serving as my frontline editor. This book has been a real family project. My inspirations and equine models live within sight of my computer workspace.

What a great job of modeling! Our little riders Connor, Erica, and Izzy are the newest generation of horse lovers. Thank you to my nephew, Ben, for bringing his guitar to model for me.

Kellie E. Anton gets credit for the great photographs. Thank you!

Tom, thanks for all your support. I know that you loved Sox as much as I did.

The song "Hillbilly Rock" mentioned in chapter 9 is Kenny Chesney's hit. It is one of the really good freestyle choices.

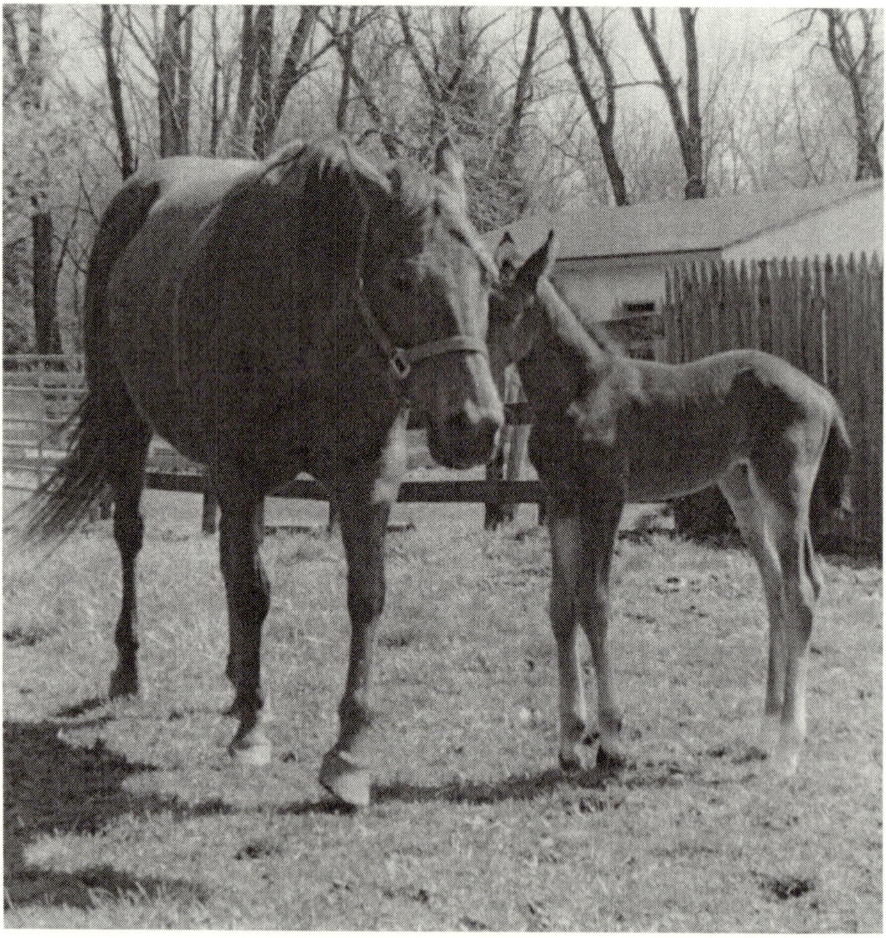

1

A NEW WORLD

It had been a long voyage, eleven months exactly, getting to here from there. My assigned quarters were comfortable, and all my needs had been seen to, but I could not wait to explore new worlds. Maybe I had cabin fever. I was becoming very uncomfortable, and my traveling capsule seemed to have shrunk. At the beginning of my voyage there had been plenty of room for me to move around, but now I felt restrained. Close to my final destination, I began to have doubts that I would make a successful landing. My environmental suit had just sprung a huge leak, and it collapsed around me.

Just as I stuck my foot through the escape hatch, I encountered frigid air. I changed my mind, and I decided to stay inside where I was warm and safe. I tried to pull my foot back in, but something was pushing on my backside and forcing me toward the escape hatch. My left leg was dangling out there, and the pressure from behind was getting stronger, but my right leg was stuck. I struggled to move it in line with my left leg, but it didn't want to cooperate. Finally I succeeded in placing my legs in a good position to escape. I stretched my neck and put my nose between my front legs, and that was when I plopped out onto the hard, prickly surface of an alien environment.

It had been hard work getting into this strange new world. Exhaustion had taken the edge off of my long-awaited arrival, and breathing in this atmosphere was proving to be impossible. A soft nickering sound from my mother reassured me, but her voice sounded different in this new world. At first other voices nickered a welcome, but their voices too were fading. My head was spinning, and I began feeling very weak. Part of my protective traveling suit that had collapsed was now blocking my air supply. The lifeline that had attached me to my mother had been broken. The umbilical cord had provided nourishment and oxygen during my long journey.

An alien sound tickled my ears, a whisper, "There is the foal; it is lying against the stall door. Open the door carefully, Bill, and pull the placenta away from the baby's nostrils so that it can breathe."

Strong hands gently removed the covering from my nose, and I took my first deep breath. Relief flooded through me. Resting from my ordeal, I heard a grunt from my mother. She had been resting in the deep straw too. She was very tired, and also weak from the effort of helping me into this world. After a little while, she rose and came close to me.

Nuzzling me and encouraging me, Mom began pushing me to stand up. Easy for her to say, she was already standing, but I was having trouble untangling my long legs. Instinct and constant encouragement from Mom made me try again. I gathered my back legs under me and shoved. "OOPS! Not quite so hard, son," my mother told me, as I tumbled onto my side. She said, "It would probably help, son, to uncross your front legs first. Try again." Three tries later, I succeeded. The effort was sure worth it! Mom guided me back to her large warm body, until I found her fresh supply of sweet milk. It warmed my belly, and it made me feel stronger.

I plopped down for a nap once my tummy was filled, and that is when the wall opened up. A chilly gust of wind ushered strange two-legged creatures into my world. They came in through an opening that had appeared in the wall, as if by magic. One of the creatures knelt down beside me, and it started to rub me with a soft cloth. I recognized its smell. It had pulled the covering from my nose, when I first arrived here. Some of my fear concerning this invasion was lessening. This creature had helped me, and the rubbing felt wonderful. Another biped was rubbing my mom and talking to her.

"You are such a good mother, Sandy," it said. Big news flash, I thought. I might be new around here, but I already knew that much. The creature turned and looked at me, like it knew what I was thinking.

"Look, Bill, Sandy's little bay colt has socks on his hind legs."

I was not sure what socks were, but I felt nothing on my back legs except the prickly straw that was my bedding. It left my mother and squatted down next to the one that had saved my life. It talked to me in a soft voice that reassured me, and it stroked my neck. I was really getting into all the attention.

Something wasn't right! A cold wet spot on my belly gave me a chill, and then it started to sting me in the place where I had been attached to my mother. The two-legged creatures left through the opening in the wall, and my momma came over to nuzzle me. She told me the burning was only medicine, and she assured me that it would go away quickly. I wasn't sure about that, but it turned out Momma was right.

I was feeling better when the two aliens returned. I scrambled to my mother's side. I was not sure that these creatures had caused the pain on my navel, but instinct told me to get up and seek the protection of my mother. Peeking from behind Momma, I watched them as they picked up the torn remnants of the traveling suit that I had worn, and removed it.

Momma said that our confined area was a stall, and the warm glow overhead was a heat lamp. Mom also told me that the light was there to keep me warm in the cold night air. I wondered what night was, but I was too tired to figure it out or ask any more questions. Yawning, I stretched my long legs out and fell asleep next to my mother under the warm glow.

A loud chorus of whinnies woke me. Blinking my eyes, I tried to focus on my surroundings. The world seemed brighter than when I had gone to sleep. Startled by a loud bang, I scrambled to my feet and scampered to my mother's side. I moved as fast as my long shaky legs could carry me. She explained that there was nothing to fear; it was feeding time, and one of the other horses just got excited and kicked the wall of its stall. The strange two-leg creatures came back into our stall. They put something called bran mash in a corner feeder. Mom seemed interested in it, but all I wanted was to nurse. One of the alien creatures filled, what mom called a bucket, with water, and it told us that we could go out to play as soon as the vet checked us.

Feeling frisky, I scampered around my mother. My legs were working better now, so I tried to run from one side of our stall to the other. They were back! The ones my mother called humans. Another person had entered with them, and he was looking my mother over. This human was a veterinarian. Mom did not mind his inspection of her, and she nickered to me that everything was as it should be. Just as I was beginning to relax, they turned their attention to me. My attempt to evade them proved futile. I hid behind my mother, but they cornered me.

He looked in my eyes, listened to my heartbeat, and checked some very personal parts of my body. A lot of attention was focused on my right front leg. A contracted tendon was his diagnosis, and I guessed that was why my right leg wasn't straight like the other one. He believed that because I was such a large colt, my leg position had been cramped as I developed inside my mother. I have to tell you that I was happy to see the backside of him when he turned to go, and I wondered how often he would invade our privacy.

Close behind my mother, I stepped from the stall—where I had been born—into the aisle of the barn for the first time, and then out through the big door. It was like being born again! Filling my lungs with fresh air, I looked around at this big, bright, new world. Mom called this the front paddock, and she told me that it was a safe place. The other horses whinnied a greeting, and mom whinnied back to them. Straining to look in the direction of their voices, I tried to focus my eyes, but the other horses were just blurry shapes to me. Several fences separated us, and Momma explained that the others were in the back paddock. The work arena took up a large space separating our paddock from the back one.

All of the new sights, sounds, and information were too much for me. I blocked out everything except for my basic needs. I was hungry for some milk, and I was ready for a nap. Most of my first day was spent nursing, exploring my surroundings, trying out my legs, and sleeping in the sunshine.

The world became clearer to me on the second day, and I was starting to get a handle on my long legs. They didn't get wobbly or tangled as much as they had yesterday. Before bedding down for the night, my mother asked me what I had learned that day. This question and answer session was to become a ritual at the end of each day. The variety among humans was the first thing that popped to my mind. I already knew that there were differences among these humans. My rescuer was taller than the other one that I encountered on my first night. That day I discovered that they were mother and son, just like mom and me. Maybe someday I will be bigger than my momma too.

A few days later, I was stretched out, minding my own business, and taking a snooze in the sunshine. Lulled to sleep by the rhythmic sound of my mom munching grass, I was sure that I was still asleep and having a strange dream. It just shows that you never know what is going to pop up to scare the wits out of you. The humans that I had met since my first day had been quiet, moved slowly, and they took effort to reassure me.

I scrambled up next to my mom and blinked my eyes. The three-board fence that surrounded our paddock had come to life! Small humans were invading our sanctuary. They stuck out along the front part of the fence line that ran parallel to the road. These scary creatures continued around the corner and lined up along the side fence that ran next to the driveway.

Until now, the scariest place in my world had been the opposite side of the paddock. It was lined with tall pine trees, which harbored dark shadows and little creatures that scurried about. Now, I made a beeline for those tall pines and their dark shadows. The pines were as far away as I could get from the strange, small humans protruding from the driveway side of our enclosure. I would have run all the way to the back fence line, but I couldn't leave Mom to face this threat alone. She was so busy eating the grass that she didn't notice the strange sight.

Mustering up all the courage that my four days of life would allow, I charged up to my mother to warn her. I bumped her head and nipped her neck to get her attention. She wouldn't budge. I explained, "Run, Momma we are in danger!"

She still didn't stop grazing. Finally, she looked up and stared at the frightening sight, but she didn't turn and run. She nuzzled me and told me how brave I was to warn her. She explained that what I was worried about wasn't a danger. They were called children, and like me they were small because they were still young.

She also explained that the squealing sound was only their way of showing the joy that they felt at the sight of me. Intrigued and a little braver, I pranced up close to the front fence where the smallest children stood. I tossed my head and arched my neck, and then I snorted at them. They squealed, jumped up and down, and clapped their hands. OK! Their reaction was a little too scary for me, so I hightailed it back to mom. She laughed and said, "They must have really liked your performance, to have clapped and cheered so loudly." It is not that I didn't believe Mom; I just wanted to test her theory. I approached the children at a walk. I got closer to them this time. I snorted and turned quickly in the opposite direction, and took off at a run. I heard them cheering and clapping, so I ran a little faster. It felt good! So I let out a couple of little hops, kicking out my hind legs. Mom praised my efforts, and she called my little maneuvers crow hops.

Mom was running alongside me. I challenged her to a race. She laughed, and told me I would have to grow a lot more and get better with my legs before I could race with her. I dreamt that night of growing big, and racing my mother across a large field without any fences.

Each day I learned something new: I learned to run really fast, I learned to stop, and to turn around. I perfected my crow hopping style, and I learned how to rear. Those were all fun things, especially rearing up on my hind legs. I would paw at the air and practice being fierce, much to the delight of the children in my neighborhood fan club. Mom would accompany me to the front fence, where she would let the children pet her muzzle or stroke her neck. I was not ready to trust my nose to them, yet.

I found out that I could charm these humans, and it was easy to get my way. Most members of my human family were easy to win over; all I had to do was nicker at them, prick my ears forward, and look cute. But cute didn't work with the barn boss. Katie was a big pain about good manners.

Before I continue, let me tell you about my human family. Bill was my young rescuer, his father was also called Bill, but my mom called him Slim. Patty is Bill's sister. Katie is Bill and Patty's mother; she is also the barn boss. Katie was in the habit of scratching my withers, rubbing my back and neck, and talking to me, while my mom was busy eating breakfast. I have to admit that I began to look forward to the back scratching routine and was beginning to enjoy it.

Emma was the newest addition to my human family. She was only eleven years old and lived next door with her grandmother. She was small like me, but her hair was red gold, almost the color of my mother's glossy coat. Most of the time her hair was braided down her back or tied in a ponytail that was almost as long as my own tail. Mom said the sprinkles on her nose were called freckles.

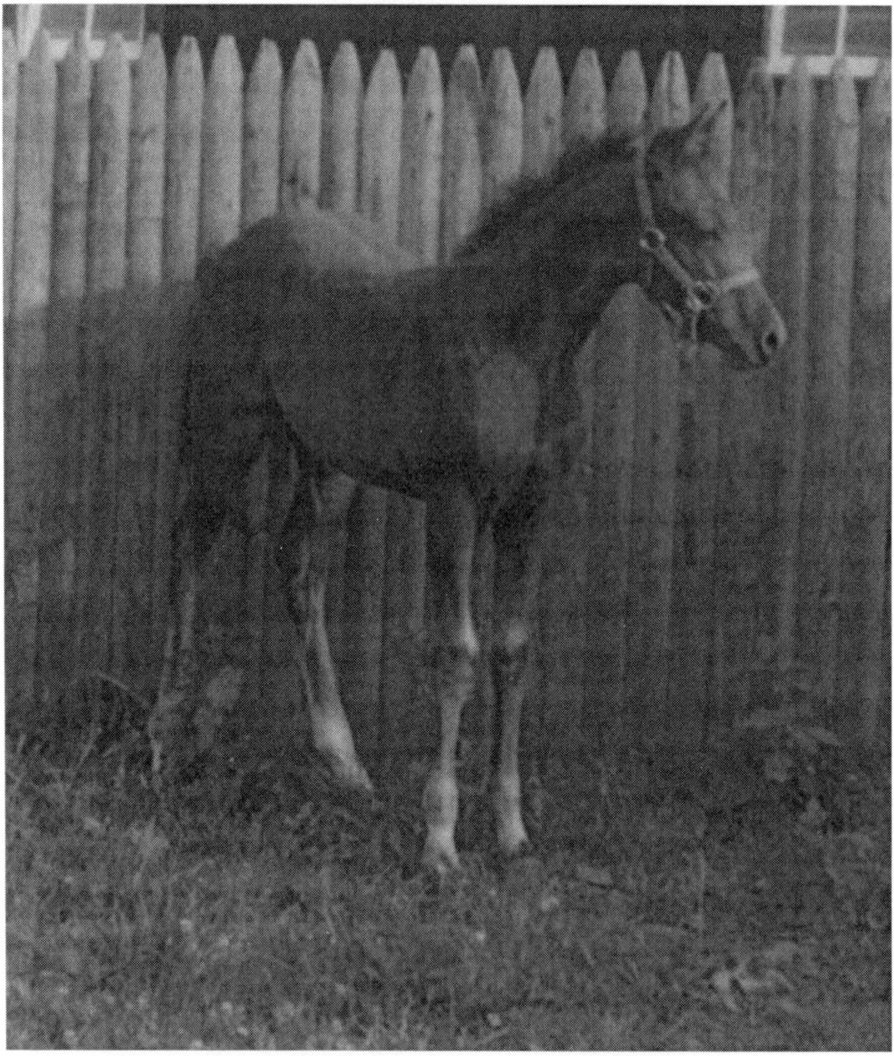

2

SMALL TOWN U.S.A.

My name is Emma, and life changed for me three years ago when my parents split, and Mom had to work full-time. I was raised in the glow of streetlights and the color of flashing neon signs. My ears were used to the hum of traffic and the voices of other apartment dwellers.

Mom couldn't get a good job that would keep us at home. So when she joined the army, we moved close to the base. That was a big change, but there were other kids who lived near us or on the base. When my mom got deployed, I came to live with my grandmother.

It is hard for me to believe that Mom grew up here; it is so nowhere! Grandma lives on the outskirts of a small town. It is really different here. There are no sidewalks or streetlights, and at night it is so quiet that you can hear the frogs and crickets. It is really creepy.

"Don't complain to your mother, Emma. She should not be worrying about us. Keep your e-mail to her happy." That was the speech that Grandma gave me along with a birthday card and a new diary. Then she told me to write my complaints down in the diary and to save them until Mom came home.

Dear Diary,

School sucks! Grandma has me dressing like a nerd, and the other kids laugh at me. I just don't fit in here, and there is no one to talk to who understands what it is like to have a parent so far away. E-mail from Mom always makes me feel better, and I know that for now, she is OK.

Dear Diary,

Today I turned eleven. Mom always told me that the trees turned colorful in October just to celebrate my birthday. She sent me a gift card for my birthday, and I tried to be positive when I e-mailed her.

I get scared when Grandma turns on the evening news, and they show what is going on in Iraq. I always look for Mom, but then I am glad I don't find her when they show the shooting. I pray every night that she is safe, and she will be home soon.

Dear Diary,

Thanksgiving is over, and I am back in school. We watched a news program that showed some of the soldiers being served turkey dinners. Mom said that she had turkey and even some pumpkin pie. Grandma warned me not to repeat that she called my dad a big turkey. I guess what upset Grandma was that I have been living with her since August, and this is the first time that he has shown up. He said that he wanted to make sure that I was doing well, but he didn't talk to me much. He ate a lot of turkey and stuffing, so did his new wife and the twins.

Taking Grandma's advice, I did not mention Dad's surprise visit here when I spoke to Mom. Instead I told her about my new reading tutor.

Dear Diary,

I could not stop thanking Mom for my new guitar. I know that I sounded crazy I just kept saying, thank you, thank you, thank you, repeating it over and over. I have her old one, with the frayed strap that is too big for me. Playing her guitar always makes me feel closer to her. Maybe we can play together when she returns.

I sure wish that she was home. The cookies that Grandma and I made got to Mom, along with the rest of the presents that we sent her. She shared her cookies with the other soldiers, and said that they loved them. Using the videocam that Grandma got us for Christmas, I strummed the notes of "Silent Night" to her. It has always been her favorite Christmas song, and I didn't make too many mistakes.

Dear Diary,

School started again, right after the huge snowstorm that came with the New Year. I thought that I was doing OK in school, but the guidance counselor didn't. She said that I have a problem paying attention. I wonder how easy it would be for her to concentrate if she had a parent in a war zone. She wanted to have me tested, until Grandma gave her an earful. The counselor said that I probably had Attention Deficit Disorder.

Dear Diary,

When Grandma got the notice from school that they wanted me tested, she marched up there and demanded to meet with the guidance counselor. Grandma informed the counselor that I had a mild case of dyslexia. Thanks to Gram, I now have a math tutor along with my reading tutor. There goes any chance of fitting in with the rest of the kids.

I guess that it was kind of funny the way that my grandma went up to the school to confront the guidance counselor. I bet that she barked orders there too. I made that bet while talking to my mother; she laughed. Still laughing, she said that Grandma could put most drill sergeants to shame.

Dear Diary,

Sorry, that I have not had time to complain to you lately. School and the two tutors keep me pretty busy. Sometimes it gets hard to squeeze in an e-mail to Mom. Guess what? The neighbor's horse had a baby! It is so cute and so tiny. I told Mom and Grandma that I never thought of horses as babies. I promised to send Mom a photo as soon as I can get a shot. It hides behind its mother and peeks out at me. The weather is kind of warm for the end of March, so the baby horse is out every day.

Dear Diary,

This is the photo that I sent Mom of the baby horse and his mother. He is not hiding behind her anymore. He races around and snorts at the kids who hang over the fence. His mother is friendly, and she will let me pet her, but the baby keeps out of reach. I am glad that I have some interesting things to tell Mom. I talk about the baby horse, or school, or the mess that I made trying to color Easter eggs. Gram didn't mind the mess that I made, and the egg coloring was kind of fun.

I don't want Mom to know how scared I am, or how much I worry about her. She told me that she was not near the bombing that was reported on the TV, but I don't think that she would tell me if she had been. I always tell her that I love her, and I ask her to be careful.

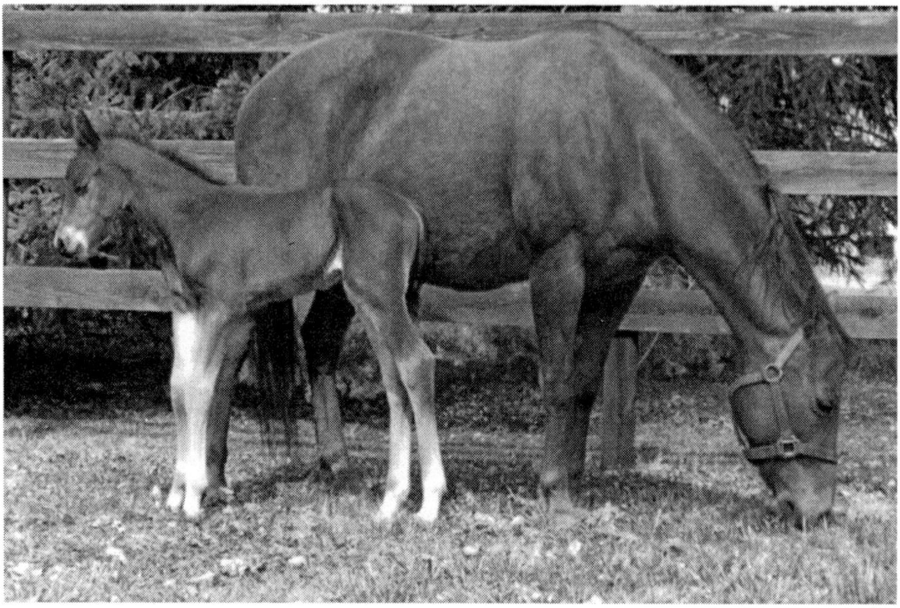

3

LEARNING THE ROPES

Katie was rubbing my neck and head, and then sneaky as you please, she slipped something over my head. Making my displeasure plain, I pinned my ears back and pawed at the stall bedding. Violent shaking of my head had failed to dislodge the offending object, laughing at my display of temper.

"It is ok, Sox. You will get used to the halter," Katie said in a soft comforting voice.

Getting into this world had been a trial, so why did I think that getting my name was going to be any easier? Momma thought that Katie chose my name because of the white socks on my back legs. I was more concerned about getting the halter off than how Katie had chosen my name. Rubbing it against my mother's side didn't work any better than shaking my head.

After I calmed down, my mother explained that the halter was like a passport, and if I was ever going to travel, the halter was a necessity. I asked why her halter did not have a tail hanging from it too. She told me that the short lead was part of my first training halter, and that later I would not require it.

"You will have a lot more lessons to learn, Sox. Rest for a little while, son; soon we will go out and you can play."

I guess that made it official, Momma had called me Sox too. So after drinking my fill of Mom's milk, I stretched out in the straw and took a nap wearing my new halter and my new name.

Bill left near the end of my first week. Two of the dogs went with him; they lived in a place called Illinois. Mom had been born in Illinois, and said that she had lived there for the first three years of her life. She said it was a long way from where we lived in Ohio. Bill was a student at the University of Illinois, and he had been here during something called spring break. It was lucky for me that he had been home on the night that I was born.

Patty also drove away, two days later. She had been home on spring break too, but from a school in Indiana. Mom wasn't sure where Indiana was, but she remembered being told that it was just west of Ohio.

Young as I am, I have to wonder about Katie's parenting skills. How could she let her children climb into those metal boxes on wheels and drive away? I had been observing these traps on wheels, as they whizzed up and down the road near the front of our paddock. They all went by very fast—some were loud and smelled bad, some were small, and some were large. Occasionally, one of them would make a loud honking noise, similar to the geese that flew over our home.

My mother said that the small boxes were called cars, and that the larger ones were trucks. Worst of all were the school buses that roared down the road and then screeched to a stop. With their red eyes blinking, they gobbled up the children and carried them away. All of these contraptions on wheels looked dangerous to me, and I planned on steering clear of them. I was just getting used to this world, and I didn't want to get gobbled up by some predator on wheels.

It appeared that the weather could be as tricky and unpredictable as the humans. Storms plagued my life and limited my playtime for the next week. Mom and I only went out for short periods of time, whenever the rain let up, but we were confined to the work arena. This fenced area was almost as large as our front paddock, but there was not a patch of grass. The ground was soft and squishy. Mom explained that the surface was sand. She also told me the rain was what had made the sand wet and squishy.

Puddles were another problem; the rainwater had pooled deep in places. Excited the first time that we got to go out again, I scampered out the door splashing mud and water on my legs and tummy. It was cold, and I did not like it much. Trying to run away from it didn't work; the harder I tried to run away the more the ground splashed at me.

On the bright side, Katie would towel me off after she removed my wet halter; and I really liked it when she rubbed my head. My wet muddy halter disappeared with her, and magically the overhead heat lamp would come on. The warm glow from the lamp felt almost as good as the spring sun.

Learning how to navigate through the mud took some practice. I discovered that I did not like to get wet or muddy. When I needed a nap, I just curled up on my mother's pile of hay, so the squishy stuff couldn't get to me. Katie and Slim must have thought my dislike of the cold wet sand and my problem solving skills were funny. At times their small chuckles or laughter would reach my ears as I napped in my dry little island of hay. Mom was patient and waited for me to finish with my nap before she resumed eating her hay.

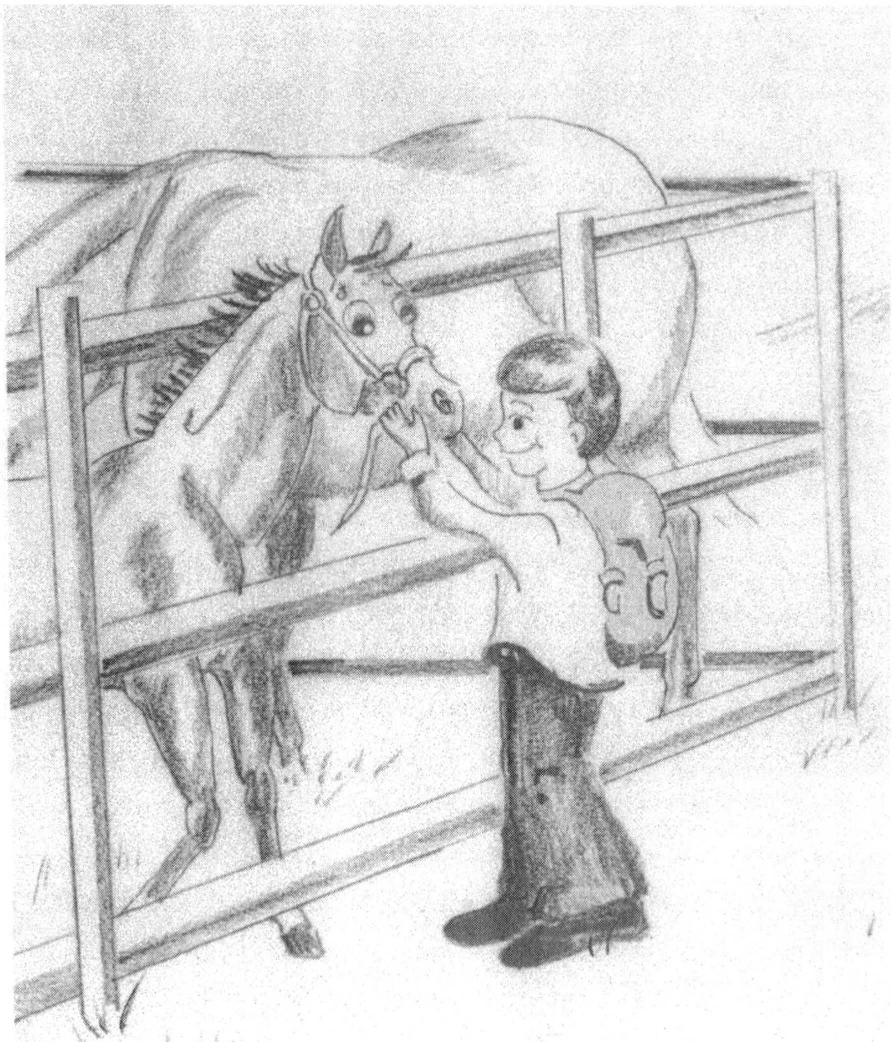

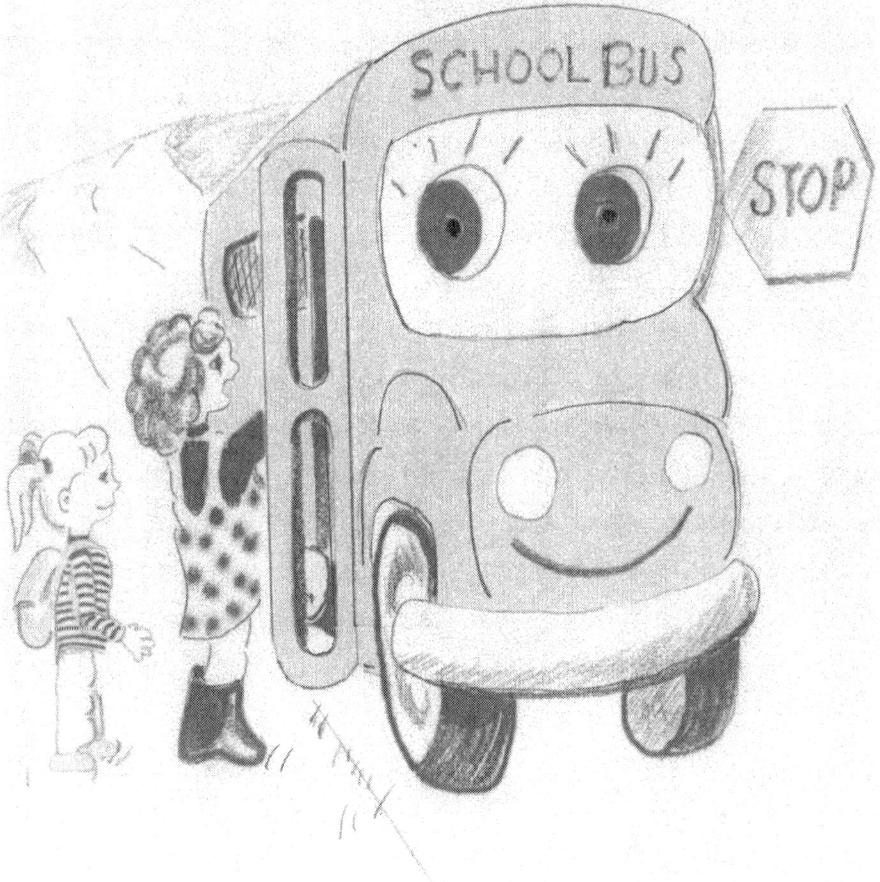
SCHOOL BUS
STOP

During my second week of life, I figured out that wearing my halter meant that I was going out to play. Heaven was the feel of a soft towel, so I stood and let Katie rub my head. I even stood there after she removed my wet halter and continued to enjoy my head rub.

Finally, Mom and I made it back to the front paddock. It was different than I remembered. Bushes and trees that had been bare—like giant sticks reaching above my head—were now dressed in green, and some wore pink or white flowers. The air was sweet with the aroma of lilacs. The road, with the noisy cars and trucks, was not as visible as it had been that first week of my life. I ran, and ran, and ran some more. I could rear really high now, and I could buck too.

Hairs prickled along my back; I could feel Katie's eyes on me. I lifted my head and stared back at her.

"I wonder what she is planning to do to me today," I said. Mom looked up at Katie, and made the comment that whatever the lesson was to be, it was for my own good.

Mom was also sure that things would go a lot smoother for me, if I didn't enjoy a fight so much. It was true that I loved a good fight. I was now a six-week-old colt, and I looked for excuses to test my fighting skills. There were not any other colts to play with, or to test my skills in mock battles. Mom wasn't very much fun, she would run for a little while in the morning then spend most of the rest of her time munching grass. Bumping her head didn't work, pulling on her halter didn't work, and nipping at her neck didn't work either. She just ignored me. So I challenged the humans.

Challenging Katie was my favorite sport. It was a little spooky, the way she had of knowing what I was going to do before I did. Instead of giving me the fight that I wanted, she would distract me, and I would end up doing things her way. Worst of all, Katie could make me think that the lesson had been my idea. During these sparring sessions, I learned how to lead, to walk and trot next to Katie. Backing was a little harder. It is not a normal thing for a horse to back up, but I learned how to do it very well.

Standing in the barn aisle next to my mother and being groomed was one of my favorite lessons. The currying and the brushing felt great. I did not like to have my feet picked up or cleaned out, but I got used to it. I was getting accustomed to being handled by Katie and Slim, and they were patient with me. The scrape of the hoof pick on the bottom of my hooves didn't bother me, and I was becoming comfortable lifting my hind legs. It was more uncomfortable for me to surrender a front leg to them, and that lesson took longer for me to learn. When my left leg was held up, it put a lot of strain on the tight tendons in my right leg, so I would rear and pull my foot away.

Two weeks ago the vet returned. He called me a super colt. By his tone of voice and the way he stroked me during the examination, I really thought that he liked me. Katie was holding my lead and scratching my withers when the vet came back into our stall. He rubbed some wet smelly stuff on a small place on my rump, and then he stuck me!

That hurt! I leaped forward and tried to get away. My effort to escape was futile. Katie and my mother just watched, while he stuck me two more times, before he released me. Backing away from them, I scrunched up my nose, laid my ears flat on my head, and glared at them. They had just let the vet come in and hurt me.

Katie patted my mom and said, "I think Sox is angry at us, Sandy."

My mother tried to make me believe that the shots would protect me from disease. I was too young to know about sickness and infection; all I knew was that shots hurt. The veterinarian was not going to catch me so easily next time. If I ever saw him again, I planned to run in the opposite direction.

A few days following the visit from our horse doctor, I had my first experience with getting my hooves trimmed. Grumpy and Goliath were my names for the blacksmith and his assistant. The other horses had been trimmed and had their shoes reset. They stood quietly through the whole process, as did my mother. Because of my age, Katie insisted that my mother and I be trimmed in our stall. I watched as Mom got her hooves trimmed, and she didn't look like she was worried or scared. Katie tied Mom in the corner when they were finished with her. Katie attached a lead to my halter, stroked my neck, and talked to me. Grumpy was looking me over and talking to Katie.

"He sure is a nice-looking colt. Too bad he is crippled. What do you want us to do with him?"

I didn't know what crippled meant, but it sure made Katie angry. She told him that I was not crippled, and the tight tendons in my right leg were already stretching. She also told him that I was going to be just fine. I could tell that she was trying to control her temper. Katie gave Grumpy instructions on just how I was to be trimmed. If there was one thing that I had learned in my short life, it was that you didn't argue with Katie. It would get you into trouble, and Grumpy

hadn't figured that one out, yet. Using the same voice that she used when I was bad, it sounded kind of like a low growl, she said, "Trim my colt the way I want, or I'll find someone who will."

I was hoping that Grumpy would leave and let Katie find someone else. That would have given me more time to get used to the idea. No such luck. Grumpy decided to do the job. He was in a bad mood, which suited me just fine. I had been looking for a good fight, and it looked like these two were going to give it to me. Grumpy grabbed a hold of my left foot—not gently like Katie or Slim—then he pushed his shoulder against mine. He knocked me off balance, and then he pulled my foot up. Rearing, I pulled my foot away from him. I pinned my ears back and glared at him.

Grumpy decided it was Katie's fault that I was fighting him. He believed that I was misbehaving because she was upset with him, and that I sensed it. I really don't think Katie believed old Grumpy when he claimed that Goliath could do a better job of handling me. With her arms folded over her chest, she stepped back next to my momma and watched me. Goliath took a short hold on my lead, and Grumpy went for my leg again.

I repeated the rearing maneuver, and I got my leg away from Grumpy, but Goliath pulled me down and roughly took a hold of my left ear, so I leaped forward and bit him. Goliath yanked hard on my lead rope and said words that I had never heard before. We fought until all three of us were sweaty and panting. They outlasted me. I was worn out, but I would be bigger and stronger the next time I met them, and I wouldn't forget.

Katie rubbed my sweaty body with a soft towel and talked to me in a quiet, gentle voice. She left us and the warm overhead light came on. I nursed from Mom, while she reassured me. Then I took a nap. I could hear Katie's parting words echoing in my dreams.

"You are a very brave colt, smart and handsome too. Someday, little Sox, you are going to be an amazing horse."

Things have been too quiet around here since my battle with the blacksmiths, and I just had a feeling that something significant was about to happen. I could tell by the way Katie was watching me that she was up to something. I was relieved when we went in for the night, and nothing unusual had happened to me.

She sprung the trap the next morning. Mom was nickering and pawing up our stall, because everyone had been grained and everyone had hay, except for us. Slim and Katie came for us and took us out to the front paddock. A huge red box on wheels was parked in the middle of our paddock. Mom called it a horse trailer. Slim walked Mom up to the back of the metal monster, and she almost ran inside it. She knew that her grain was in there, and she forgot all about me! I called for her, but she ignored my frightened cries. Katie tried coaxing me closer by offering me some grain. She knew that I liked it and had been eating quite a bit of it lately, but I was not interested in food. I was worried about Mom. Cautiously, I stuck my head in the trailer, and I called to her.

Preoccupied, trying to gain my mother's attention, I had forgotten about Katie. Moving behind me she had locked hands with Slim, and together they pushed my rear end forward.

I jumped up and scrambled to the safety of my mother. Once I calmed down, I realized that I was inside the metal monster, but nothing terrible had happened. So I began to relax and nurse.

Breakfast in the trailer was repeated for several days, and by the end of the week I was following Mom into the trailer. Magically, doors had appeared on the back of the trailer during the second week of my training. It looked a little different, but it didn't concern me. What did worry me was the truck that was attached to the front of it, but after a few days I didn't even notice it anymore.

One day the doors closed behind us, and I felt a rumbling in my feet and up my legs; the monster was moving! Mom sensed my panic, and reassured me.

"Calm down Sox, we are just going for a ride." Too frightened to think of a good question, I just asked, "Why?" Like all mothers, Mom seemed to know just what to say.

"This is the way that we can cover many miles in a short time. Riding in the trailer is an adventure, Sox. You never know where your travels will take you." We went for more rides during the following week, and getting in and out of the trailer became just another lesson learned.

Mom and Katie agreed that I was smart, and they were impressed with how quickly I learned most of my lessons. My manners received mixed reviews: Mom was pleased with me; she said that I was bold, curious, and brave. Too bold, too curious, and bad mannered was Katie's assessment of me. Just because I liked to rear and nip occasionally, she was worried about me around the neighborhood children and the youngsters who came for lessons. As my basic training progressed, Katie became more focused on improving my manners.

Around and around I ran inside the small round pen, while Katie rode Mom. I wanted to be out there in the big arena too. When Katie finished working with my mother, she made me go around the pen on a long line. Lessons in walking, stopping, standing still, and reversing direction on command were not difficult for me, but running was my favorite sport. I ran around the paddock, and I ran small circles in the round pen. All of the exercises that Katie and I did, as well as the long days spent outdoors, had worked wonders on my right leg. The tendons were stretching, and my small handicap sure didn't slow me down any.

Another month had passed by before Katie began to lead me next to my mom, while she finished up their ride. It was strange to be led by a mounted rider, and I was not allowed to play. Only four months old, and I pranced beside Mom just like the grown-up race horses pranced next to their pony horses. As Katie and Mom taught me to pony, I listened to her talk to my mother. "We are going to have to wean Sox soon. You are becoming much too thin, Sandy. Look at the bite marks on you, and the scratches where his hooves have struck you. Sox needs some discipline; you really shouldn't let him climb all over you. He will get in trouble if he tries that behavior with the other horses. I think it is time you and Sox join the others. We will try putting the two of you in this arena for a little while, so he can get used to them. He has to learn his place before we can wean him."

Close, the other horses were huge! Measured by weight and something called hands, Mom was—to my surprise—a small horse. She weighed about a thousand pounds and only stood 14.3 hands at the withers. Golden highlights sparkled on her sorrel coat when she trotted to the back of the sand arena to greet the other horses. This was a new and exciting experience. I had not been this close to the other horses that lived at our little farm. Usually, I was separated from the others, and I gazed longingly at them from the confines of the round pen, or from the more distant front paddock.

Blinking my eyes, I tried to focus on the approaching horse. Just a silhouette stepping out of the setting sun, she came closer at a leisurely pace. Continuing to blink, I watched the large white mare touch noses with my mother. I was sure that looking into the sun had played tricks on my eyes, because she had spots all over her white body. She was built much like my mother, with a powerful chest and muscular hindquarters, but she stood four inches, or one hand, taller than Mom. Despite her build, I don't think that she was a Quarter Horse like us. Not one to be shy, I stuck my nose through the fence boards to sniff at her, but she turned and walked away. Mom said that her name was Gunner.

Our next visitor was a tall black mare. She too touched noses with Mom, but unlike the other mare, she also touched noses with me and nickered a greeting. Her name was Tar. A large bay horse kept his distance but looked us over. I asked my mother why that one didn't want to meet us. She said, "He is an old gelding, and he knows to stay away from a mother with a foal." I found out later that he was called Handy.

Little did I know that Katie had been watching as I was introduced to the other horses, or that she was going to let Mom and me join them. I was about to find out that Katie was not the only one who thought that I had bad manners and that I needed an attitude adjustment.

Dear Diary,

Grandma said that I could take horseback riding lessons, if Mom agreed. I started by telling Mom how great I thought Katie was. It turned out that Mom knew her. Sometimes I forget that Mom grew up here, and that it was my dad who was from the big city. Mom said yes. I can take lessons!

That is the good news. The bad news is that Mom's last e-mail was very short. Something is going on, because we have not had a videocam link for almost two weeks. Usually, she answers my e-mail the same day, but now her mail is delayed for days.

Dear Diary,

Grandma helped me pick out the animated Mother's Day card that I sent Mom's e-mail. I got another short message from her. She thanked me for the card, and she wanted to hear about my riding lessons.

It was easy to answer her question about whether or not I liked my riding lessons. I had just one word, yes. I had only had two lessons, but I loved it. I told her about the big white mare with all the spots that I have been riding. Her name is Gunner, and she is twenty-one years old. I guess that is sort of old for a horse. I thanked her for letting me take the lessons.

After getting all mushy and telling her that I thought she was the greatest mom in the world, and that I loved her, I told her how very fast the baby horse is growing. His name is Sox.

Dear Diary,

Only a couple more days of school left. I have been spending a lot of time next door on the weekends and after I finish my schoolwork. Katie said that she could use some extra help around the barn, and in exchange I could ride more. I just had to get permission to work around the barn and the horses.

Grandma said that it was OK with her, as long as I kept my grades up. I e-mailed Mom a copy of my school report. I think that my grades are better, but I am waiting to hear what Mom has to say about my grades and about working in the barn.

It is scary not knowing where she is, or when she might be able to answer me.

4

SHOT DOWN BY GUNNER

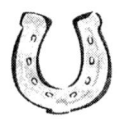

Following breakfast we were turned out, as usual, Mom and I in the front paddock and the other three horses in the back. Everyone had been settling down to some serious grazing after getting the morning run and bucks out of their systems. Then, I guess that Katie felt it was safe to let Mom and me out with the other horses.

Excitement got the better of me, and I ignored my mother's warning to stick close to her. The large white mare with the many spots came up to greet my mother, but once again she ignored me. She fascinated me. I pranced up to say hello, but she continued to graze and ignored me. Shaking my head and rearing high, I placed my front hooves over her back, the same way I did with Mom when she ignored me. Like lightning her back leg flashed out, and she sent me through the air. She looked over her shoulder and warned me.

"Watch your manners, little brat, or you will come to a bad end."

I picked myself up from the dirt, along with my dented pride, and I went in search of my truant mother. A string of curses came from Katie's lips that singed my little ears as I went sailing through the air. If you have ever hit your elbow and felt a sharp pain run up your arm, then you know just how my hip felt.

The pain was easing, only to be replaced by a numb feeling. It was as if my back leg had gone to sleep; I couldn't feel it.

Finally, I spotted my mom and I hobbled up to her. I had expected some sympathy. Continuing to graze she said, "I told you to stay close to me, Sox. Not everyone is as indulgent as I am with your rowdy behavior and your bad manners." I was crushed. Momma had never criticized me until then!

Not much intimidated me, and I was always looking for something or someone to challenge, but a lack of information could get a guy killed! I might have waited to introduce myself if had I known that the white mare was the herd boss. Mom called her the alpha mare. She also told me that the white mare was known as the Gunner.

Something that I need to explain, Gunner was not her real name, but one that she had earned. She was a deadly shot when she took aim and kicked out with her back hooves. Lucky for me that she had only used one hind leg.

My hip was sore for a few days, but I was still able to run and play a little during the same day that I had been shot down. I kept close to Mom for a few days, and I made sure there was plenty of room between my small body and the Gunner. Katie, however, was pleased with my intelligence, and gave credit to the Gunner for the quick improvement in my manners.

Life got a lot more interesting as spring turned into summer and the numbers of riders taking lessons increased. Trucks pulling two horse trailers, four horse trailers, and horse trailers of many different colors brought strange horses to our farm several times a week. From my round pen or the front paddock, I watched as Gunner, Tar, and Handy joined the schooling sessions. The horses carried young riders around the arena.

Fascinated, I watched the older horses go through lessons with their riders. Some of the instructions that Katie gave them, I understood. Walk, trot, whoa, and back were familiar to me, I could do those things. Other maneuvers or instructions were unknown to me, but I found them entertaining.

Not even a little entertaining was the occasional absence of my mother. Alone in our stall, I frantically whinnied for her. When she returned, I would ask where she had been. Her answers varied, sometimes she had gone to a 4-H workout, and other times she went on something called a trail ride. Workouts and trail rides didn't keep her away too long, but horse shows would take her away from me for half of the day. It never occurred to me that Katie was deliberately separating me from my mother, and getting me used to being home alone.

Emma was the bright spot in my day. It worried me that my little friend often rode the Gunner, but the crabby old mare liked the humans. Emma helped me make it through the stress of weaning. That was what the humans called it when they took your mother away from you, "weaning."

I looked forward to my time with her. Emma talked to me, or played her guitar and sang little songs to me. One day she told me, "I know what it is like to miss your mother, Sox. My mother is a soldier, and she is far away from me too."

One day my mom had said, "Sox, I think that you and Emma are kindred spirits."

"What does that mean?" I had asked, afraid that it was something awful. "Spirits are like ghosts. Right?"

Her eyes twinkled. She gave me horselaugh, and then she said.

"A kindred spirit is another being who has a lot of character traits in common with you, and the two of you are able to communicate without a lot of effort."

It was one of many times that I was not sure what my mom was talking about, but I was relieved to know that ghosts were not involved. A few days following our talk about kindred spirits, Mom went away. I missed her company and her wisdom, as well as the comfort of her sweet warm milk. There was no one to answer my questions, or reassure me while she was away.

Dear Diary,

June is almost over, and I am riding a couple of times a day! Katie said that I am a natural horseperson. I think that the patterns that she gives us to practice controlling our horses are helping me to focus and follow directions. It is so much fun. I even like cleaning tack and sweeping the barn floor.

Little Sox is not very happy. Katie has started working his mother more, and when Sandy goes on a trail ride or to a 4-H workout, he cries and paws up his stall. It calms him and he likes it when I talk to him. So I park my stool in front of his stall and I talk to him while I clean the tack.

I am counting the days until Mom's deployment is over. I wish that she could see me ride and that I could just give her a big hug. Grandma told me that Mom used to ride too! Mom never told me about that.

Dear Diary,

I sent Mom an e-mail to wish her a happy Independence Day. It is becoming harder to keep my worry from her. I wish that I knew where she was going that she would not have an internet connection. I promised that I would write to her by snail mail, but somehow that only makes it feel like she is farther away.

I am visiting with Sox more often. Katie took his mother to another barn to separate them during the weaning process. Poor Sox, he is so lonely. I know just how he feels.

Dear Diary,

I thought that old people were supposed to be forgetful. Grandma doesn't forget anything! She reminded me that I was behind on my summer reading that she insists on. It was part of the deal we made for me to ride. One book a month over summer vacation didn't sound too bad. She wants me to read the three of them out loud! Then, she suggested that I practice reading the books to Sox. I know that he likes me to talk to him and he loves the sound of my guitar, even when I make mistakes, but I don't read well. The words on the page get jumbled up, and the harder I try the more jumbled they get.

Dear Diary,

Sometimes I don't think that Grandma trusts me. She has been reading the books too, and I was given two choices. Write out a summary for each book, or tell her the story and read one chapter from each book out loud for her. HELP! Reading to Sox was one of Grandma's better ideas. He didn't care if I got stuck on some words; he just liked to hear me read to him.

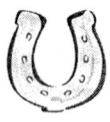

Because Katie was busy with lessons and horse shows, she paid less attention to me. On my own too much, I looked for trouble. My care and training exercises were assigned to Patty and Emma. Patty was home for the summer, and I found that she was easier to get along with than Katie. Patty looked like Emma's big sister. Their hair color was almost the same, but like me Emma had brown eyes, and Patty's eyes were blue. She taught Emma how to work me on the

lunge-line. I liked to work with Emma. She was always happy when we got something right. So I tried real hard to do my lessons correctly.

Mom returned a month after she deserted me, and I was very happy to see her. I called to her, but she would not answer me. She pushed me away when I got too close or tried to nurse.

"You are not a suckling foal any longer, Sox. You are six months old now and a weanling. It is time for you to be independent," she told me. We did not even share a stall anymore.

Mom still watched out for me, and she continued to teach me the things that a horse should know, but it was not the same between us.

Emma, Patty, and I continued our training, and showmanship was more difficult for Emma and for me than our other lessons had been. Emma learned by practicing with my mother, who had been a champion youth horse.

Patty and I got real good at standing square. I learned not to move when she walked from one side of my body to the other. I trotted at her side, I learned to walk, stop quickly then turn one hundred eighty degrees, and trot off in the opposite direction. It was hard not to puff out my chest and prance when Katie let us join one of the showmanship lessons. It was exciting working in the arena along with the other horses. I messed up some, but I got better each time, and I could tell that Mom was proud of me.

Dear Diary,

Summer is streaking by. Streaking, that is pretty good! Don't you think? Grandma bought me a dictionary and a thesaurus. She has to help me read the dictionary. Sometimes the definitions are pretty hard for me to follow.

Dear Diary,

I went to the fair with Patty. She showed me the 4-H exhibits, and we toured the decorated 4-H horse barns, the dairy cow barn, the beef cattle, and the goat and sheep barns. At every stop we ran into people who knew Patty, and she introduced me to everyone.

I was ready for a break when we took our elephant ears and lemonades to the bleachers. Munching and slurping on my fair treats, I watched the flag ceremony that started the afternoon 4-H horse show. I have to admit that I was jealous of those lucky kids.

Dear Diary,

I got a letter from Mom today. It was dated July 8. That was six weeks ago! So I guess that she has not received the one that I wrote her last week. I hate this. Six weeks to get a letter? That is like living in the Stone Age. I don't like not knowing where she is or waiting so long to hear from her.

I have so much to tell Mom. I am riding Sandy now, and Katie will let me show her. That is if it is OK with Gram and Mom. Gram said that I could, until I got the final word from Mom. I ended my letter to her with a plea. SAY YES! SAY YES. PLEASE, SAY YES. I had written it in big bold font, but Grandma thought that it was overkill, and she made me tone down my request to just capital letters.

On a sunny morning, I got a bath, and I had my hooves polished. Mom and I were served breakfast in the horse trailer. Mom and Emma were off to a late summer horse show, and Patty decided to take me too! Emma won third place with my mom's help. The excitement, the strange horses, and the loud speakers made me nervous. I could not stand still. All of the things that I had learned at home just fell out of my head, to be trampled under my restless hooves. Patty tried to make me feel better.

She said, "Don't worry Sox; it won't be so bad next time. You will get used to it." Patty took me along whenever there was room in the trailer. Emma, like me, made mistakes, but she continued to improve too. Mom rarely talked to me at a show; she was totally focused on the task at hand.

Having Patty and Emma for company helped ease the desertion of my mother, but then they deserted me too! I felt lost and alone. Patty had disappeared and gone back to college. Emma still came to see me, but not as often, or for as long. She was in school most of the daylight hours, and she could only visit me on the weekends.

Green bushes near the house turned bright red as the weather got colder. Our trees turned red, orange, bright gold, and then brown. Leaves covered the grass; they crunched under my hooves, and I had to paw through them to reach the quickly disappearing grass.

Then came the white! It covered everything. It clung to all the trees. It stuck to the fence, and it hid the grass under its winter blanket. Putting my nose in it, I found out that it was cold, and if I snorted it blew up into my face. Handy, the old gelding, explained that the cold white stuff was called snow. It was my first winter, and I hadn't realized how long it would last.

December made Emma sad because her mother would not be home to spend Christmas with her.

"Sometimes I can talk to her on the Internet, but it is not the same as having her home. I really miss her Sox," she told me.

I did not have a clue what the Internet was, but I liked it when she talked to me. Like a good friend, I listened, I nuzzled her, and I allowed her to hug me when I thought that she needed the comfort.

A few days after Christmas, it snowed and it snowed; some of the drifts came up to my tummy. When the snow stopped, we built a snowman in the front paddock. Actually, Emma built the snowman, and I ate its carrot nose. Funny thing about that snowman, whenever I would eat his nose he grew a new one by the very next day. Carrot Nose made Emma smile. She took photos of me stealing his nose, and Katie took some pictures of Emma, me, and Carrot Nose. She gave them to Emma to share with her mother.

When the winter winds were not howling, I could hear the faint music of Emma's guitar drifting into the barn. The music sounded sad, and my heart ached for her. I wondered if she felt as lonely as I did.

Dear Diary,

I still do not have an answer to the last two letters that I sent to Mom at the end of August, and I have been back to school for two weeks! In the first letter I told her about the fair. The second letter was to brag. At my very first show, Sandy and I won third place in a showmanship class of twenty other kids. Wow! I was so pumped that I couldn't wait to get home and write to her.

I explained that I did not place in the walk trot class, and the experience was more like the dodgem at the amusement park. When Katie is instructing us at home, she must also play the part of a traffic cop. Most of my first riding class I guided Sandy around stalled or balky ponies, and tried to avoid being run into by horses that were not guided very well.

Dear Diary,

October came and I still had not gotten another letter from Mom. I was getting really scared, but Grandma told me that no news was usually good news. She explained that letters often got lost or delayed because they passed through many hands. She said if something bad happened to Mom, the Army would notify us. I prayed that Grandma was right.

Dear Diary,

Late in October I got a birthday card from Mom, but still no answer to my letters. We did not hear from her until she returned to Internet land just before Thanksgiving. That is the good news. The bad news is that her tour had been extended, which meant that she could not come home for Christmas. So again this year, Grandma and I baked cookies, we bought toiletries and a few useful gifts, and we shipped them to the Middle East.

Dear Diary,

It snowed hard after Christmas, and I tried to shake of my sadness by playing in the snow with Sox. Grandma watched us from her window, while we built a snowman in the front paddock between our house and Slim and Katie's house.

Sox got in the way more than he helped, but he was having fun licking and biting at the large, round snowballs that formed the body, I would roll one, and he would stick his head in the way to check it out. The funniest part was his reaction to the snowman's nose.

I went into the house to get a large carrot. Sox waited for me right where I had climbed through the fence. As soon as I put the carrot nose in place he swiped it, and then ran off to munch on it. I brought another carrot with me, along with my digital camera, and as soon as I replaced the nose he stole it again. This time I was able to capture him in my camera.

I attached the photo of Sox to my next e-mail to Mom, and ended up with more than the one photo that I had planned on. While I was busy taking snapshots of Sox, Katie had been photographing both of us. She sent the photos to my e-mail, along with a photo she had taken of Sandy and me with our first ribbon.

Dear Diary,

Finally, I talked to Mom on the videocam. She congratulated me on my first ribbons, and she said that she got a good laugh out of the snowman photo. I told her that I replaced the carrot every morning, and Sox would steal it the first chance that he got.

Dear Diary,

It is already the end of March, and today is Sox's first birthday. Only a year old and he is bigger than Sandy! Mom said that I could join 4-H. Katie is going to let me use Sandy for my project horse. I am so excited that this year, when I go to the fair, I will be one of the lucky kids showing a horse.

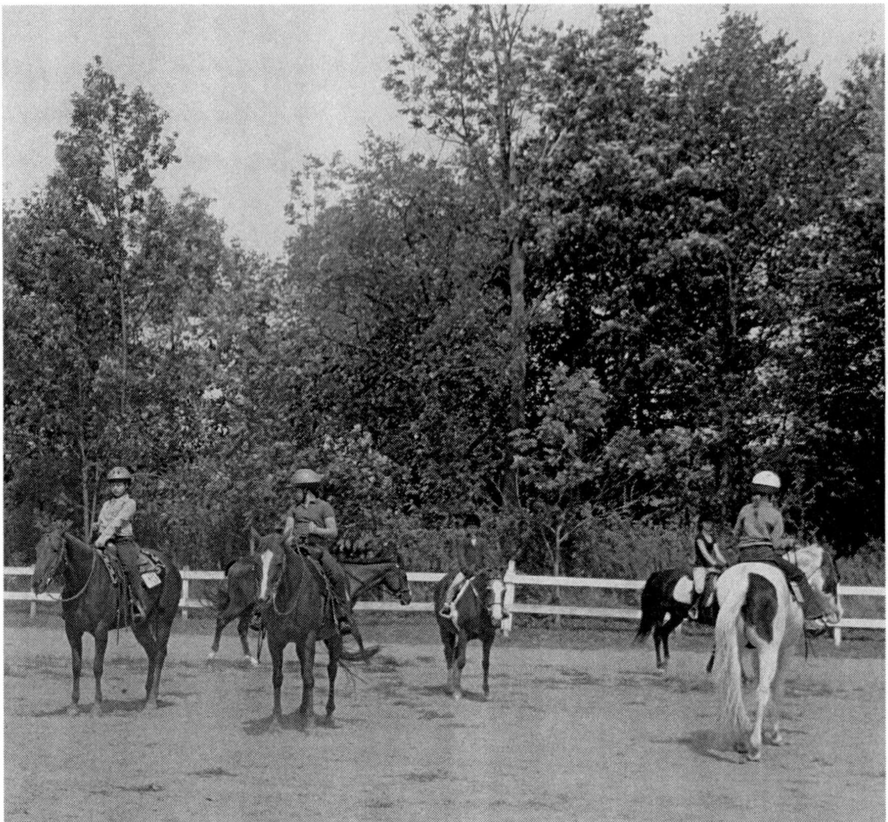

5

NEW HORIZONS

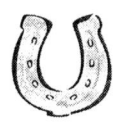

I became a gelding in the spring, and everyone commented on what a better mannered horse I had become. The tendons in my right leg had stretched, and to most people the leg looked normal. It still gave me some trouble after a long trailer ride, but it was getting stronger every day.

I was one now, and in the horsemen's world I was called a yearling. During my yearling summer I accompanied Emma and my Mom to shows, and as a pair they were advancing rapidly. Emma was showing Mom in riding classes, and they were leading the walk trot division for beginner riders in the thirteen and under age group. I was very proud of them.

Horse shows are very interesting places, and I went to a lot of different shows as a yearling. I met some little horses called minis. Mini is a nickname for miniature horses. Minis only come up near my shoulder. On the other end of the spectrum are the draft horses and the warmbloods, the giants of the horse world.

4-H shows and local schooling shows expanded my limited view of the world. Some of the shows we went to were only for registered American Quarter Horses, and most of the horses there looked very much like Mom and me. Many miles rolled by beneath my hooves as I rode in the big red horse trailer.

Late that summer I got my first saddle. I wore it proudly, as Katie or Patty worked me in the round pen or on the lunge line. Sometimes one of them would pony me along side my mom or the Gunner. Working alongside the Gunner for the first time was a little scary, but she was all business, and I made sure to mind my manners. It was hard for me to believe that I had only arrived here last spring. I had learned so much. I was an accepted member of our small herd. I had a human family, and I had my friend Emma.

Dear Diary,

I haven't talked to you since March because I have been really busy. I still have two tutors, but now I am grateful for them. They help me when I get stuck on a school assignment, and my grades are improving too. I have to keep my grades up to spend more time at the barn and on my 4-H horse. That is so fun to say, "My 4-H horse."

I think that I finally found a place where I fit in. 4-H is where I have found kids with the same interests. The kids in our group range in age from eight to eighteen. There are thirty of us in the Rainbow 4-H Club. We have meetings once a month at Katie's house. She is one of three advisors for our group.

Most of the time I ride Sandy, but during summer vacation Katie has me ride one or two of the other horses too. Sandy always gets the day off after a show or after she gets her shoes reset. On those days I could end up on Gunner, Handy, or Tar. Sometimes I worked one or two of them, or I just might have to warm them up for a lesson with a younger rider. Other times I would end up cooling them out. I love every minute that I spend on a horse.

Dear Diary,

I am thankful that we began by showing at local schooling shows. Sandy has a lot of experience in the show ring, and she never makes a bad move in showmanship. So all I have to do is make sure she is in good condition and well groomed. That is the easy part. Reading, remembering, and following the patterns are the hard part. Because Sandy and I travel to the horse shows with Katie, I have her and Patty to help me figure them out.

Dear Diary,

The Quarter Horse shows were a reality check for me. I was beginning to fill the bulletin board in my room with ribbons. I even had a few trophies on my dresser. The first time I went in a showmanship class at a Quarter Horse show, I was overwhelmed by the sparkles on the clothes.

Katie made me sit and watch some of the older kids show. She critiqued them the same way that she did for her students and for the kids at the 4-H workouts. I started to see past the fancy clothes and look at the showmanship. After the morning that I sat with Katie, I began to watch the older age groups that followed my class at the local and 4-H shows.

Patty told me that she used to watch the older age group, like I was doing, and it helped her to copy down the pattern for the class that she was watching. She told me that many times, if the first person in the class messed up on the pattern that everyone after would mess up too. She was right; a lot of the kids didn't remember the pattern and would just follow what the horse in front of them did. It really helped my confidence to know that other kids made mistakes too. So far, I have not missed a pattern. It had worried me that if I missed my pattern that everyone in the class and those who watched on the rail would know that I was dyslexic.

Dear Diary,

Sandy and I won our division in showmanship at the fair, and placed fifth in our age group in western horsemanship. We placed third in western pleasure. I had such a good time at the fair that I could not wait to come home and tell Mom.

Big surprise! I got off of Sandy following the pleasure class, and then Grandma came up and gave me a big hug. She even patted Sandy's neck. I did not know that she was at the fair or that she was watching me show. Maybe Gram is not as tough as she makes everyone think; I thought that I saw tears in her eyes. I didn't say anything. She would have just said it was the dust or something.

6

JUST SAY WHOA!

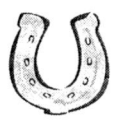

During my two-year-old fall, my training as an athlete began in earnest. Once I was comfortable with the weight of a rider, Katie would guide me around at a walk and trot, and then she would make me stand still. Standing like a statue was the hardest part for me. If practice makes perfect, then I must be perfection.

I understood what whoa meant from all of my groundwork. Groundwork is what I had been doing since I was a baby; it is the most basic training. Many days of halter lessons, lunge line training, and endless lessons in the round pen made it easy for me to understand what Katie wanted from me. Most horses have three gaits: the walk, the trot, and the canter. I was mastering all three gaits on command.

Standing quietly at home while she gave instructions to her student riders was easier for me than mastering the same task in the show ring. Over and over, we were the last horse and rider team to exit the ring. My skin was too tight! I was sure that I was going to burst out of it. Quivering from ears to tail, I waited impatiently to follow the other horses. One by one they began to leave the lineup. Some would go forward, one at a time, to collect the fluttery little ribbons. Horses that didn't receive ribbons would head for the exit gate, except for me. We horses are heard animals, and I wanted to go with the others, but there I stood alone in the center of the arena, until Katie decided that it was time to go.

I went along to all the shows as a two-year-old. Katie rode me around while she coached the young riders. I traveled to 4-H shows, open shows, schooling shows, and a couple of Quarter Horse shows. I was there for all of them. Katie just rode me around, and once in a while she rode me in walk-trot class, and it was in those classes that I learned to stand my ground. Several times Katie and I stood there and watched the other horses exit the show ring. Sometimes we would stand there long enough for another class to enter the opposite gate.

Walk-trot classes are beginner classes, and they are usually for riders under ten, but some shows have walk-trot classes for older age riders or green horses like me. I was a little worried the first time that I was called a green horse, but my mother assured me that I was still a bay. I was relieved that green was not my new color, but green horse only meant that I had very little riding experience.

Emma was progressing faster than I and was doing a super job of learning how to ride. Mom became Emma's 4-H horse, and as a team they were hard to beat in showmanship, horsemanship, and trail classes. Emma had mastered showmanship back when I was only a weanling. Horsemanship or equitation was the rider's ability to communicate with their horse. Often a horse and rider were asked to perform a pattern, and they were scored on how well they performed the maneuvers. Mom loved the trail class; it offered obstacles for a horse and rider to negotiate, and they were scored at each obstacle. Some obstacles included the crossing of a bridge, walking over poles, or walking through a water hazard. I was content to be a spectator and let Mom and Emma compete in that class. Some of those obstacles looked a little spooky to me.

Like me, Emma was growing and changing. She was thirteen and almost as tall as Katie. She still read books to me and played her guitar for me, and I noticed that her voice was changing. My voice was changing too. I didn't sound like a foal anymore; now I had a big powerful voice.

Usually things slowed down once the children returned to school in the fall, but not this year. By the end of August, I was wearing a horse blanket, and in October I left home for the first time. At first I thought that we had gone to another horse show, but as time went by I realized that I was there to stay. Thankfully, my mom was at the boarding stable too. At the time I did not realize that I would spend many more winters there. We made excellent use of the large indoor arena, while Katie continued my training through the long winter months.

I was sure that Katie had lost her mind. Our workout was almost over when she rode me straight at the arena wall! We had been working at a trot, but she would not allow me to turn away. It was a good thing that I had not been going very fast, because I bumped my head, and she said, "Pay attention Sox, and you won't bump your head."

We ended every workout that way, and soon I was able to stop straight. I never bumped into the wall again. I also figured out that if I sat down some and brought my legs under me that I could stop better. Katie praised me whenever I got my back legs under me. When I heard her say whoa, and I felt her sit back a little in the saddle and take her legs off of me, I stopped. Whoa meant stop!

By my third birthday I could run up to the wall and slide to a stop. I was doing pretty well sliding to a stop in the center of the arena too. We had spent a lot of time practicing my circles.

The right circles seemed harder for me than the left ones, but they were getting close to the same size and shape.

During my rest periods, I watched Emma work with Mom. I was amazed at how fast my mother ran toward the wall, and then she just slid to a stop that sent the dirt flying up behind her. I could not believe this was the same horse that I could not get to run with me, until the day I picked up a stick and chased her with it.

A rainstorm had knocked down some tree limbs during my yearling summer. Out of boredom, I had picked up a long twig and had begun to play with it. Running with the twig in my mouth and shaking my head, I noticed that the other horses were running away from me. It had always been a challenge for me to get the older horses to play, so I would search for a nice long twig once I learned that it resulted in a gallop around the paddock. Maybe the other horses thought that it was a whip or a snake. That was the fastest I had ever seen my mom run until today.

Emma's face turned a little green, like she might be sick. It took her a few more tries to get used to the feel of Mom's powerful burst of speed and her equally powerful stop. I don't think Emma believed that Mom could move so fast or stop that hard. Mom had always been a quiet little pleasure horse, but she sure knew how to raise a cloud of dust when she was called to the task of reining. Katie was happy with Emma's circles, so she asked her to roll Mom back over the hocks and circle the opposite direction over the same circle that she had just made.

I watched as Mom galloped her circles and ran straight down the arena into a sliding stop that sent the dirt flying higher than before. I am ashamed to admit that I was jealous of my mother. I wanted to run too, but Katie would not let me. She would tell me, "Easy, Sox. We need to gather all of the ingredients before we can bake a cake, and then it has to set before we add the icing." Sometimes the things that Katie said didn't make any sense to me, but I twitched my ears back and listened to her voice. I still dreamed of running and running as fences dissolved before me. I knew there had to be open spaces out there somewhere, places where horses could run free mile after mile, but the wide-open spaces were only in my dreams.

As a three-year-old, trail riding was added to my exercise routine. I was like a country kid on the first trip to a big city. I gazed around in awe. Huge trees linked their branches high over my head, and rays of sun filtered through the thick summer leaves. At first I was hesitant; I waited for the cue to turn, but it never came. I walked for miles without encountering a fence. My dream of no fences had come true, sort of. In my dream I did not have a rider, and I was free to go as fast as I wanted to.

Emma's mother returned home just before my fourth birthday. I was happy for my friend, but I missed her and my mom at the horse shows. Emma stayed home, and she only showed Mom at 4-H shows. However, I was not given a lot of time to feel sorry for myself. Katie and Patty had teamed up, and they decided to take me to some reining shows.

Ohio, Pennsylvania, Michigan, Indiana, and Illinois rolled by beneath the tires of my new slant horse trailer. Riding on a slant was much more comfortable for me than riding straight in the old red trailer. The gently rolling hills of Eastern Ohio made my mouth water, as I watched all that delicious green grass roll by my window. The rolling hills became steeper when we entered a place called Pennsylvania.

Going to shows in Pennsylvania was a lot more tiring than traveling north to Michigan, or west through Ohio to Indiana or on to Illinois. Up and down we went, lean to the right then quickly lean to the left, it must be like riding the big coasters at Cedar Point that Emma told me about. She made the whole experience sound like fun, but I found it difficult to keep my balance.

I met horses that lived in the foothills. I met horses that had traveled to the shows from farms high in the mountains. They were used to straddling the floor of their trailers the way that a surfer balances and walks his surfboard. I guess that like surfing big waves, it takes a lot of practice to balance over mountain roads. I got better at trailer surfing, and after my first trip into steep hills and the mountains, I never mentioned the balance issue again. I did not want the other horses to think that I was a wimp.

A big part of my balance problem was because of my new sliding shoes. Sliding plates were wider and smother than the shoes that I had been wearing on my back feet. When I stopped quickly, the plates helped me slide over the dirt or sand, much like skis let humans slide over snow. As a result my stops were improving, but the slide plates made it harder to keep my balance in the horse trailer. It was much easier to keep my balance when we traveled through the flat states to the north and west of our home.

I wondered how the barns and houses kept from falling down the steep hills. I noticed that entire towns were perched on the sides of the steep slopes. Roads wove through the green landscape like gray and brown ribbons. I pondered the living conditions as I peeked through my window at the passing towns and farms. Were the stalls floors in the barns steep too, like the land around them? I missed not having my mother along. She could always be counted on to answer my questions without laughing at me.

I had two pilots at the reining shows. Patty warmed me up then entered me in the green horse class, where she could use two hands to guide me. Katie showed me in jackpot gelding, and later in the season she included me in the novice open class. I was progressing and perfecting my maneuvers. Katie got real emotional the first time that we rode a penalty free pattern. That was the first time that I placed at an NRHA Show, and we won money. Katie called it getting a paycheck. NRHA means the same as the National Reining Horse Association, and there are approved reining shows in all the states that we traveled to.

Emma and Mom joined us for the Quarter Horse show on Labor Day weekend. Hanna, Emma's mother, came too. Hanna looks like an adult version of Emma. Hanna is home from the army to stay, and Emma told me that her mom was studying to become a nurse. My friend was a lot happier since her mother had come home. She and her mom played their guitars for us every evening of the three-day show. The music and songs sounded a lot happier than the sad notes that had filtered into the barn during my first winter. Labor Day was the last show of the summer for us. As usual, Emma and Mom placed in every class they entered. They won the youth reining and the youth trail class. They finished up the weekend as high point youth rider in the fourteen and under age group. I am not sure that I was the most proud of their accomplishment, but I was right in the running with Hanna and Katie.

It was a milestone for me. I will always remember that show. Patty and I won the amateur showmanship class and the amateur horsemanship class. We also entered the amateur reining. I knew that we were in a reining class as soon as Katie put splint boots on my front legs. I had begun to wear skid boots on my back legs to protect my fetlocks, and they were securely in place too.

All eyes were on me when Patty rode me into the arena. In reining, the horse and rider can't hide in a crowd and hope that the judge won't notice a small mistake. Unlike pleasure classes or even the horsemanship class, in reining only one horse at a time enters the arena to perform the required pattern.

Patty walked me down the center of the outdoor show arena. Along each side of the arena were three red cones. We walked past the first cone; when we reached the center cone we turned to the left, and we stood in the center facing the left wall. Seated on either side of the center cone were two people. Katie had told me long ago that one of these people was the judge and the other one was a scribe. The judge never took his or her eyes off of me. Every move that I made was given a score. The judge called out the score for each skill that I performed to the scribe, and the scribe kept track of how well I did each maneuver.

Every horse enters the reining pen with a score of seventy. If I could perform the maneuvers correctly and not make any mistakes, I could keep my seventy score. Performing a skill or maneuver poorly would subtract from my score, but excelling at a maneuver would add to my score. Boo boos and bad behavior would also be subtracted from my score. Bucking, striking, kicking, or biting is bad behavior, and five points are subtracted for each offense. Boo boos are things like forgetting to change your lead, or breaking to a trot, and overspinning up to one quarter of a circle. These offenses fall in the penalty box on the score sheet, and they can subtract one half of a point to two points from the original seventy. If a horse bucked, the judge deducts five points, and the horse's score is now sixty-five.

I stood facing the judge and waiting for instructions. I remember thinking that Patty was confused because she always rode me with two hands in a reining class. She had me on a loose rein, and she was using only one hand to neck-rein me. Maybe she thought that this was another horsemanship class because that is the way she was riding me. When she urged me forward, I played along with her and moved into a canter to the right. Three circles to the right, then we stopped at the center again. I made four spins to the right, and then cantered off to complete three circles to the left.

This time when we stopped at the center, Patty asked me to spin four times to the left, and then we started to the right again. When I returned to the center, she urged me forward, and we changed direction. Changing direction meant that I had to change my lead while moving. When I make a circle to the right, my right legs reach out further than my left ones. On the right circle I was on my right lead; now I had to change my leg position at the center so that my left legs would lead me around the left circle. Changing my lead legs while cantering or galloping is called a flying change of leads.

Lead changes always get me a little excited, so when I came to the center again I picked up a little more speed. It was still more difficult for me to go from the left lead back to the right one. I gathered my legs under me and turned to the right. This time Patty turned me at the top of the right circle and rode me straight at the opposite side of the arena. I ran down the centerline of the arena, and then I felt Patty pull her legs off of me and say whoa.

I gathered my back legs under me, and I slid so far that my front feet were in danger of being run over by my back ones. Whew! That was an unnerving stop! I thought that I was going to flip over. It is a good thing that I figured out how to move my front feet out of the way.

Patty turned me sharply to the right, so I rolled to the right and I ran back the way we had come, retracing our tracks. I knew what was coming now, and I picked up more speed. This time when Patty said whoa, I slid longer, and I flung dirt into the air. Spectators whistled, and hooted and clapped, much louder than the children had when I was just a little foal. I knew that they liked what I had done, so when I completed my left roll back, I ran hard at the opposite end of the show pen. Patty had to yell above the thunderous applause after our last stop and our back up to where we had begun our pattern at the center of the arena. "GOOD BOY, SOX," she said, and she patted my neck.

Do not ask me what my score was, because I do not know. It is strange, but the Quarter Horse shows don't announce the score. At reining shows we knew our score as soon as we finished our run. Katie smiled at us and she said, "That was a beautiful run with very few mistakes." Our ride earned second place. Placing did not mean a lot to me, but the fact that everyone was happy about what I had done, including my mom, was real important to me. Patty and Emma took turns hugging my neck and patting my shoulder and rubbing my head. It is a good thing that I don't have a problem with public displays of affection. Emma even gave me a big juicy apple.

The day after the show, I enjoyed the rest. In the morning I ran and bucked some; I rolled in the grass and looked for apples under the trees, but more than one day of rest was too much for me. I was ready to go back to work.

TRAIL RIDE! I was having trouble standing still long enough for Katie to wrap my legs. She had used words like a well-earned rest and a short vacation when we returned from the horse show three days ago. Katie had always wrapped our legs when we traveled, and the wraps were old news. But I was ready to explode with pent-up energy, and I felt like I was going to jump out of my skin. I knew that I was going on a trail ride when Slim brought Gunner out of her stall. She was his favorite trail horse. I guess that there is just no accounting for some people's taste.

Hinckley was a little more of a challenge than some of the other trails that I had traveled so far. There were a lot of hills to climb, a steeped banked creek to cross, and just enough flat trail skirting a couple of fields where we could canter a long way. I wondered how I could get Katie to buy me a set of earplugs. Gunner just shattered my left eardrum, she kept shouting, "HEY! Is there anybody out there that I know?"

Here was the problem, if no one answered her she kept calling, and if someone did answer she only got noisier. Since we were traveling side by side, I got the full blast. It was much quieter when Slim rode Handy or Tar. Gunner only went on short trail rides because of her advanced age. Twenty-five years old was ancient to me; after all, my mom was fifteen. I guess if we were related that Gunner could be my great-great-grandmother. On that ride she settled down after the first hour.

I had come to love the parks and the trail rides. The best part was that I could travel for miles and not have to retrace my steps. We mostly walked or traveled at a slow jog trot, but Katie encouraged me to extend my trot up the hills. Some of the reiners that we met from other parts of the United States called it a long trot. So I long trotted up the big hills, and I walked down them. We jogged along the winding parts of the trail that wove snakelike through the trees.

Occasionally, deer would travel through the trees and underbrush along the trail. They were as curious about us as we were about them. Squirrels scampered up the trees, and they scolded us for interrupting their work. They were busy collecting acorns to store for the winter.

Gunner surprised me. The old mare never backed off. When I long trotted up a steep hill, she was right with me step for step. When the trail broke from the cool dark cover of the trees, it wound its way around two sides of a large field. This is the spot where Katie allowed me to canter. Today there were deer in the center of the field, and when we began to canter, the deer took off at a run. Gunner must have thought that a gallop was called for, and she whizzed past me.

In a flash, she put least ten horse-lengths between us, and she was turning the corner to the longer part of the trail that skirted the field. My blood ran hot, and every muscle in my body quivered. It took a few seconds for me to realize that I could run after her. Katie bumped my sides with her legs, and she said, "Go get her, Sox."

I was running! Dust billowed in my wake; as my legs gobbled up the distance between us. I was so high on running that when I caught up with Slim and Gunner, I ran right past them. Katie let me run for a while, and then she began to slowly rein me in. We stopped at the other edge of the field and waited for our trail companions. Slim and Gunner caught up to us. Gunner was breathing hard when she said, "You can really move Sox, but I bet I could have beat your little socks off when I was your age."

A match race between us at an equal age would have been close, but I did not care if she thought that she could have beaten me. I was just happy to hear her call me Sox instead of brat, so I let her boast pass. Sometimes, you just have to let the old horses have their fantasies.

Trail rides became part of my training schedule. We rode the trails two or three times a week for the remainder of September. In October the trees turned to vivid colors, and by the end of the month their leaves covered the trails.

Deer became more visible when the frosts stopped the growing season. As the grass and wild flowers disappeared, the deer came closer to the trails looking for food. Their coats were changing too. Fawns lost their spots, and their coats became thicker and darker as they prepared for winter.

I wondered what the deer living in the parks ate during the winter. The deer that lived by us traveled along the riverbanks, and they could be seen in farm fields or backyards that were close to the rivers. During the winter they would come into our paddocks at home, and they would eat any hay that we had left. When the grass stopped growing, Katie threw hay out for us, and the deer ate our leftovers.

Weekend trail rides were more fun because Mom and Emma would join us. Emma's mother came with us sometimes, and Hanna usually rode Tar. On the first weekend of November, we had just started across the river when a large buck crashed through the trees and chased a smaller male deer into the river on the opposite bank. Outmatched and terrified, the little buck leaped from the riverbank. Running toward us, I could see that his huge brown eyes were bugging out of his head as he kept his focus on his enemy. Our presence went unnoticed. The young one was too busy escaping the bigger buck to see that we were in his path. Katie hollered for the other riders to let him through.

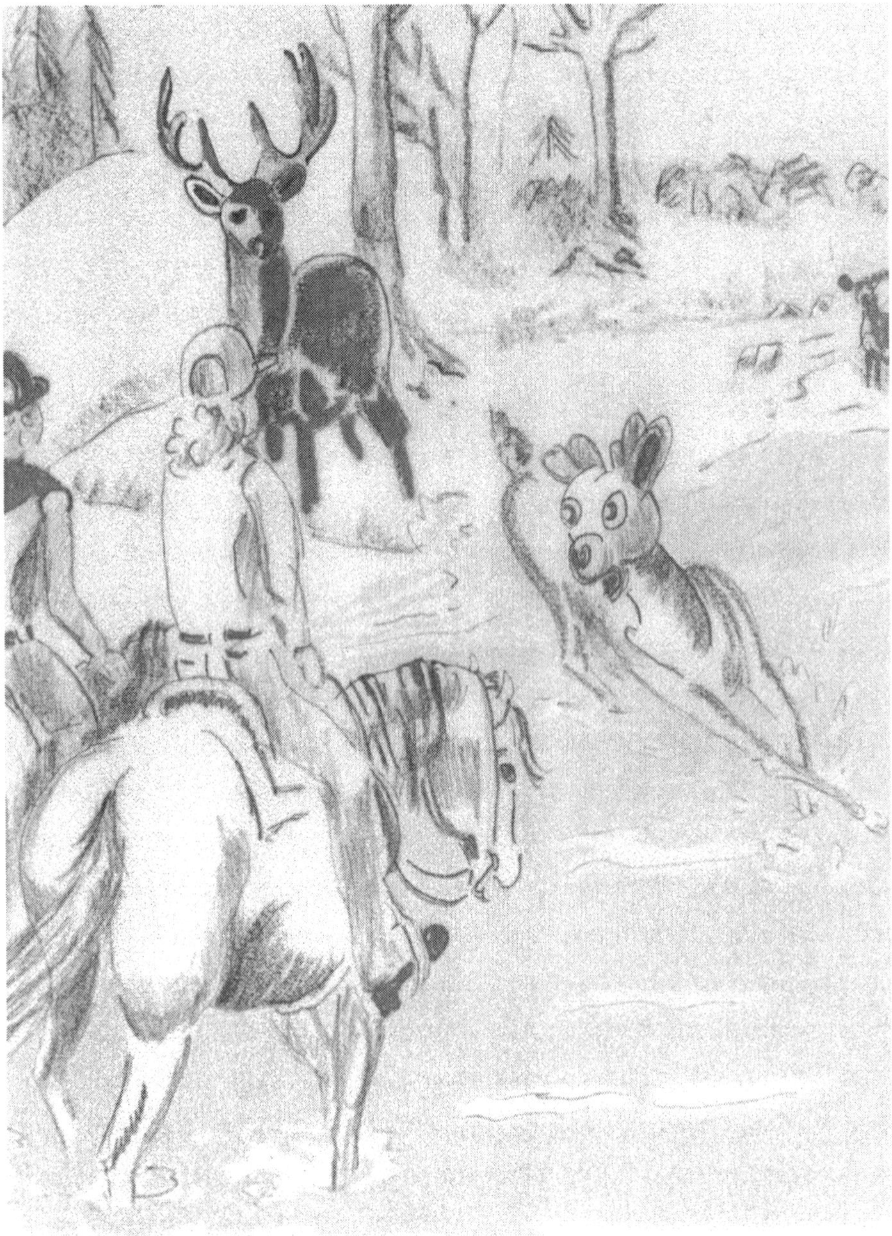

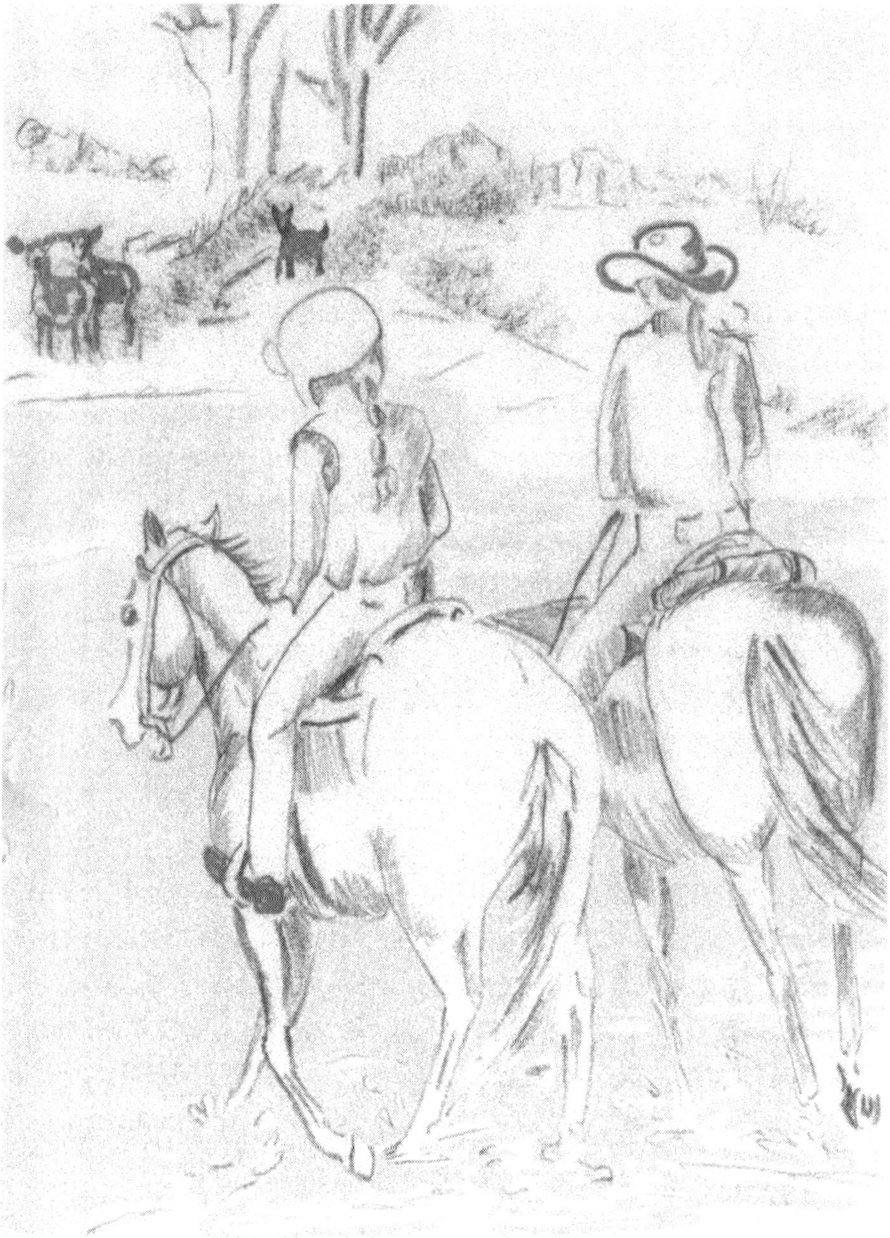

Mom and I leapt to the right, while Slim and Hanna rode Handy and Tar to the left. It was a good thing that we moved to let him through and lucky for all of us that the water was not very deep. We were able to move quickly out of his way. Still, it was a narrow escape. I think that terrified little buck would have crashed right into us.

Climbing up the opposite bank, I kept my eyes and ears tuned for the sights or sounds of more crazy deer. Handy and Tar were ahead of us when Mom asked me, "Do you remember the first time that you saw a buck, Sox?"

I didn't answer. I just snorted my disgust, and she laughed. Why do mothers always bring up dumb things that you do when you are little? It is embarrassing. It was just before my first winter, about this time of year, and I made the mistake of asking Mom, "Why do some of the deer have trees on their heads?"

She laughed and then told me, "Those are not trees on their heads, Sox. What you see on their heads are antlers." She also explained, in between snickers, that only the bucks, male deer, have antlers. Four years have passed, and my mom still has to bring up little kid mistakes.

My final trail ride for the year came the following weekend. Fortunately, we never encountered any more panicked deer. It was a good thing too. The river was getting trickier to cross. Crossings were in shallow water, but it was freezing, and ice was forming along the edge of the banks. Scattered puddles also wore thin coats of ice, and it crunched under our hooves. Snow began to fall on the ride back to the horse trailer, and I could tell by Katie's big sigh that this would be our last trail ride for a long time. I was disappointed.

Mom perked me up. She said, "A horse can negotiate trails or work in the snow Sox, but not with slide plates on their back feet. You are a reining horse in training, and that makes you special." She went on to tell me that less than three percent of all horses excel at the sport of reining. Mom claimed that reining was in my blood, and that I came from a long line of working cow horses and reining champions. She sure had a way of making me feel invincible.

So I left the park trails behind, and I plunged heart and soul into the next phase of my training.

Photo by Tim Finnegan

7

ICING THE CAKE

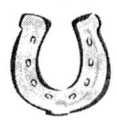

I spent my third Christmas at the boarding stable. Santa brought me a new winter blanket, and the fuzzy red stocking that hung on my stall door. My Christmas stocking was filled with carrots, dried apple slices, and peppermints. The treats lasted for a couple of weeks, only because Katie miserly doled out only one or two per day. Mom was stalled next to me, and I noticed that Emma was not as stingy with her treats.

Katie had always monitored what I ate, and she made sure that I got plenty of exercise. I liked Katie, but she was the human equivalent of my mother. She was always training or teaching me something. She scolded me when I was bad, but she praised me when I was good. Whenever I got sick or when I hurt myself, Katie took care of me. I trusted her, but Emma was my best friend. We had both grown up. In the spring I would be five, and Emma just had her sixteenth birthday.

After Christmas, my training became more difficult and demanding. I worked hard to perfect my spins, my rollbacks, and my sliding stops. Back when I was just learning to spin, I would get dizzy if I had to do more than two or three spins. Now, I was capable of six or seven speedy rotations. I could stop right where I had started my set of spins or add another one quarter of a rotation when the pattern called for it. Shutting down my fast spins when Katie told me and hitting the correct spot took a lot of practice.

In the beginning of my training, I struggled with my right spins. It felt natural for me to plant my left hind leg under me and to spin around it to the left. Crossing my right front leg over my left and pushing my body to the left was easy. It took me a long time to learn to cross my left leg over my right leg, so I could spin to the right. Now I was able to spin really fast in both directions. No one could tell that I had ever had trouble with my right front leg.

I concentrated so hard on my lessons that I did not have time to daydream about running; at night I slept dream free while I recharged for the next session.

By the end of January, I was hunting my circles. Hunting a circle is reining talk for staying on a circle until told by your rider to do something else. I could perform this task on a loose rein. Katie seldom used two hands to guide me anymore. We communicated with a light rein laid against my neck, her leg against my side, or a slight shift of her weight in my saddle. I could see that Katie was pleased with my progress.

However, I was not sure what she meant when she said, "You are doing an excellent job Sox. All of the ingredients in place, and we are ready to finish. What do you say? Shall we put the icing on the cake?" I didn't really know what she was talking about. I did not know anything about icing. Emma had let me lick some sweet stuff from a piece of her birthday cake, but I am sure that she had called it frosting.

WOW! Icing meant speed! Many hours, days, and years had passed while Katie taught me the basics. Always, she kept me at a slow pace and taught me to be calm, even when she added my reining maneuvers. She had never let me run in the arena or the outside work pen. After our gallop in the park, she checked my legs a couple of times a day. Her strange behavior had lasted several days.

At first I was not sure what she wanted, but I remembered the smooching sound that she made from my early training. She would make that sound and pop the whip behind me when she wanted me to run faster on the lunge line or in the round pen. Going along at a brisk canter and hunting a large circle, I picked up a little speed. Katie did not try to rein me in. Instead, she bumped me with her legs and moved her hand forward. That was all the encouragement I needed. I had been waiting my whole life to run, and as long as I stayed between the reins and continued to hunt the circle she let me pick my speed. I ran as fast as the confines of the indoor arena and the large circle would allow.

When I began to slow down, she shifted her rein hand back and said, "Easy Sox," and then she guided me into a smaller circle. Finished with the left set of circles, heart pounding and sides heaving, we stopped in the center of the arena. Large billowing clouds of my own breath obscured my vision. I sucked the cold winter air into my lungs and waited restlessly for the next command.

I was ready to run some more, but Katie made me stand in the center of the arena and rest. Running got me revved up, and I was having trouble standing still. Finally, she let me move again, but it was only to walk. It seemed like forever before we started on the right circles. This time, when Katie moved her hand forward and smooched at me, I ran like the wind.

By my fifth birthday, I was able to run large circles at a gallop, and I could shift down to a slow lope or an easy canter when Katie asked me. Through the winter, I learned more reining terms and their meanings. I learned that a reining pen was much the same as a show arena. Fencing was what they called it when you run straight at a wall.

At the first winter clinic we attended, several horses bumped their heads. I had learned that lesson when I was just a colt, and I never repeated the same mistake. Clinics made me restless. I got bored while the humans conducting the sessions talked and demonstrated the maneuvers.

I liked the winter schooling shows more than the clinics, but Katie never asked me to really run like we ran at home. The winter shows allowed us to perfect my skills and to develop our timing as horse and rider.

In the middle of March, we went to a schooling show to practice some more. The show pen was smaller than the arena at our boarding stable. It was only about half of the size that I was used to, but I was able to gain enough speed that it was easy to see that I had slowed down for the small circles. Doing rundowns and rollbacks was harder. I was only able to run about five strides before I had to stop and run back the other way.

Spins were easier to accomplish, but the spectators who were hanging over the rail enclosing the show pen distracted me. I missed my cue to shut down my right spins, and I way overspun. Oops! I just blew the class. My overspin was good for a big fat score of zero. Reining horses are not allowed to make mistakes that take them off the designated pattern. I was supposed to do four spins, not four and a half. So Katie made me do them again before we left the show pen.

We had one more chance at it, but when Katie rode me into the small arena this time, she was using two hands to guide me. At the end of the rundowns, instead of rollbacks, she made me spin, and where the spins were called for in the pattern I shut down right on the spot. Emma was waiting for us, and she wanted to know why Katie had gone off pattern.

Katie told her, "The reason that we are here, Emma, is to practice and to work out any problems. Sox had trouble concentrating with the crowd so close. He missed his right shutdown in our first class, so I chose to school him." Then she gave Emma some pointers. "You need to ride Sandy like it is a horsemanship class. The arena is small, and the ground is sticky. You are not going to be able to slide. So just go for correct form."

I stood there, out in the warm-up area, covered from head to tail with a blue blanket called a cooler. I stood with Katie and Slim and watched. Emma and Mom were up next. I held my breath when they entered the arena. They started their large circles at a soft canter, twice around to the right, and I was worried about how they were going to slow down for the small circle without breaking gait. Breaking gait means dropping to a trot from a canter or a lope. Back at the center of the arena, Mom shifted gears, and she went into the most ridiculously slow lope that I had ever seen. It was like slow motion. I snorted and shook my head at the sight. Katie laughed and she told me, "Don't worry, Sox. You don't have to go that slow." I was relieved, because I did not think that I could do it. Still, sometimes it was creepy the way that Katie knew what I was thinking. Slow motion Mom won the amateur reining! That was the same class that Katie had used to school me, after I messed up in the open reining.

Dry now, I had my winter blanket on by the time Emma and Mom entered the youth reining. Their run was really looking good, and they just had the last rundown to go, when a little dog jumped from its owner's arms right in front of my mom. Emma pulled on the reins to stop Mom.

It was a good thing that they were traveling along at an easy canter. Mom was able to stop and back quickly to avoid squishing the little dog. I watched in disbelief as the dog's owner charged into the arena to save her pet. The little black poodle wore a plaid coat that matched the one on the short round lady with the blue white hair who was trying her best to capture the little critter. Mom stood taking in the strange sight. The dog was having a great time! Now three more spectators followed by the ringmaster entered the arena and joined the chase. One small dog playing tag with five people had hijacked the horse show. When the dog had enough exercise, he sat down and waited for his owner to pick him up and carry him out of the pen.

Because her run had been interrupted, the judge told Emma that she could have a rerun. I could tell that Katie was proud of Emma when my friend refused the judge's offer. She told Katie, "I thanked the judge, but I told him that my horse had done a good job, and that we were finished for the day." Boy! I thought that all the practice in the world couldn't prepare a horse for some things. You just have to do the best you can.

A light snow fell on our backs as we walked up the ramp into the trailer and headed for home. A short time later, and a few miles up the interstate, the snow turned into sleet. It made the roads icy, and it slowed us way down. Fifty miles south of home, we ran into heavy snow. The trip should have taken us about an hour. Instead, three hours later we pulled through the drifts that blocked the drive at our winter boarding facility. We unloaded in snow that drifted almost to our bellies.

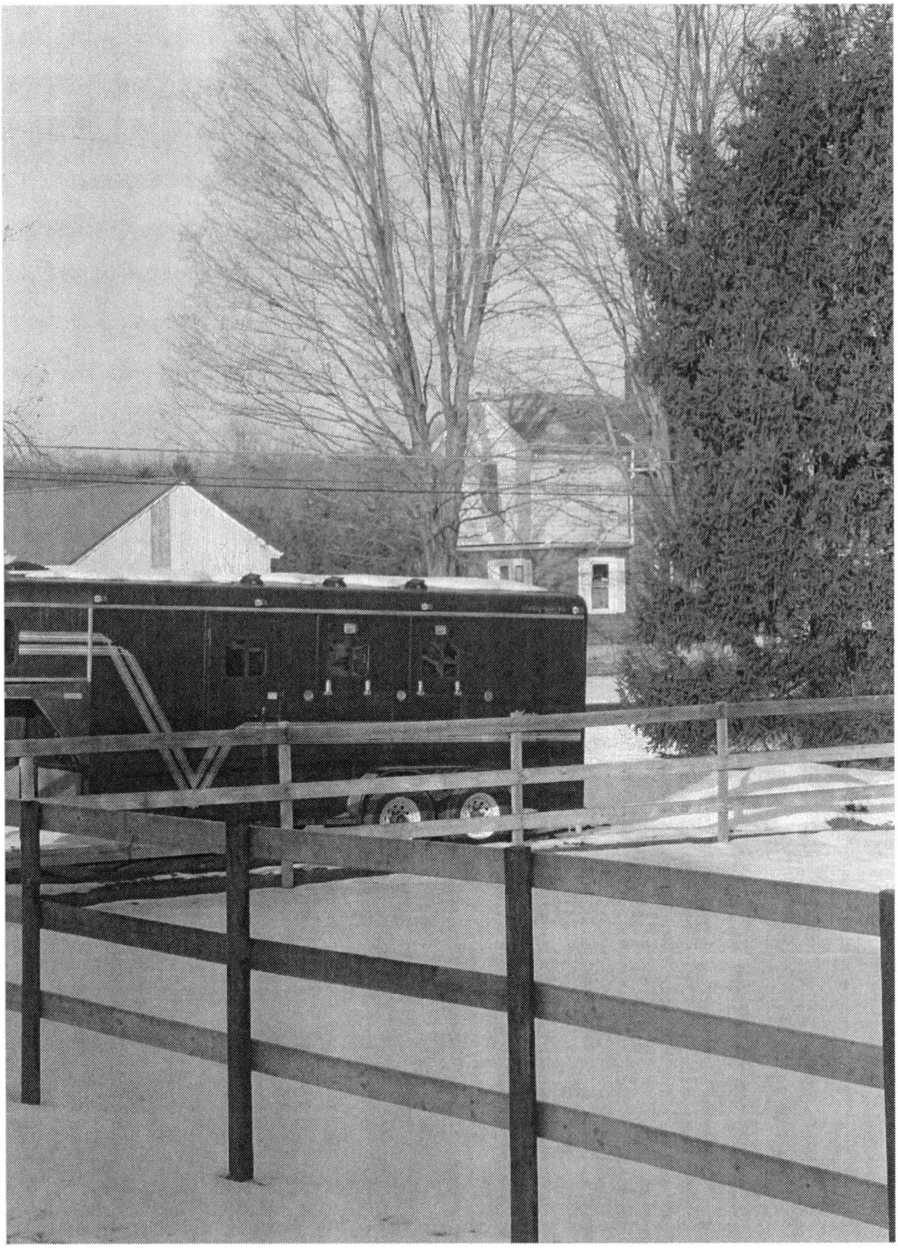

8

THE STORM

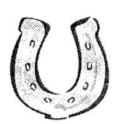

Maybe the early schooling show had been a warning that we all missed. The snowstorm that we ran into after the little dog fiasco was only the beginning. Our first NRHA outing that year was in Western Ohio, and we got caught in another snowstorm on the way home.

Mom disappeared a few days after Easter. At first I thought that she had gone to a show, but the horse trailer came home without her. Emma rode the Gunner to continue her riding progress, and she rode me to practice her reining. Like me, Emma had grown a lot, and she was taller than Katie, but their stirrup length was about the same. So it made responding to Emma's commands easy for me.

A trip to Michigan was next on our agenda. In the first weekend of May, I was traveling alone, and I sure missed my mom's company. I also missed my little friend. Emma had stayed home to feed and turnout the other horses. After eight boring hours, I was unloaded in a freezing rain. Slim and Katie unpacked, while I watched from a cozy freshly bedded stall. Grain and hay were supplied, but I was more interested in what they were doing than eating. I hoped that they were not going to disappear too! I watched them closely while they set up the tack stall. The storm raged all night, and the air was colder here than it had been at home, so I wore my winter blanket. Slim, Katie, and our dog Buddy, kept me company on that outing. The other stall held my feed and tack, along with the human show clothing. Slim rolled out a piece of carpet before everything was moved in. It was a comfort to me when they curled up on the cots, and Buddy settled down on the old saddle pad that was his horse show doggy bed. I knew that they would stay with me, and I began to enjoy my grain.

I scored my first seventy in Michigan. Katie and I had been flirting with seventy for a while, we would score sixty-nine, sixty-eight and a half, or sixty-nine and a half. She was so happy that you would have thought that we had won the class. The weather had gone from cold and rainy on Friday night, to hot and steamy by Sunday afternoon when we packed up to go home.

We stayed home for the next two weeks, and Emma rode Gunner more often. Katie rode me three days a week. Emma rode me every other day, three or four days a week. The practice was fun, and we were getting real good at our communications. Our reining maneuvers were awesome! Katie told Emma that she could show me next year, because my mom was going to have another foal in the spring.

Mom returned a few days later, and she told me stories of the big farm that she had visited. Many Quarter Horses lived there. Visiting mares like my mom were kept separate, and many of the other visiting mares had foals with them. Emma resumed her riding schedule with Mom. Because Emma was still in school and she did not have time to ride me, I felt left out.

Katie worked me harder and more often. It was as if she knew I was feeling abandoned. She rode me every day. Sometimes she rode me twice a day, and we started to ride the park trails again. I looked forward to trotting up the big hills. She loped me for miles, and she let me gallop on the long straight parts of the trails. I liked to work, especially if it required running! I could run for miles or cruise countless circles and barely break into a sweat. Strong muscles rippled under my glossy bay coat. I was ready to take on the world, and more than one day off made me restless.

Patty went with us on our next trip. Slim stayed at home to take care of the other horses, and he was at work when we pulled out of the drive and headed south. Patty was taking her new horse along. I was in the center stall of the horse trailer, sandwiched between my mother and Patty's new gelding, Mack. Mack was a registered Quarter Horse too. His coat was only a little lighter than Mom's sorrel coat, but he had a cream-colored mane and tail, so the humans called him a chestnut. They also said that he had lots of chrome.

Chrome? I was confused. I thought that chrome was the shiny trim on cars and bicycles, but I did not know what chrome was on a horse. So I asked Mom. She said, "I think that chrome is what they call his white markings." Mack had a white star on his forehead and four white stockings. The socks on my back legs only reached up to my ankles, but Mack's stockings went almost to his knees in the front, and they ended just below the hocks on his back legs.

Most of our Friday morning was spent grazing, while our humans gathered up our saddles, hay, and grain. They packed a lot of other stuff too—human clothing, food, and other things that I was not sure about. Mack, Mom, and I got a bath before we left for the show. The weather was warm enough for the bath to feel fantastic, but an hour down the road the heat in the trailer became uncomfortable. Katie pulled over at something called a rest stop; she opened the hinged windows to let us stick our heads out. We all greedily drained the bucket of water that she gave each of us, and then she snapped the screens in place. We were on the road again. Thankfully, she left the windows open. More air came through to cool our backs and to circulate the air in the trailer better.

I knew that we had arrived when I saw all of the other trailers and heard other horses. Nervous whinnies and loud pawing echoed from surrounding horse trailers. I understood their complaints. It was hard to suck the hot, humid air into my lungs. The trailer was stifling even with all the windows and doors open. There was no longer a breeze to cool our backs. Manes plastered to our wet necks as we stood in a pool of our own sweat, and we began to pant. It had only been a few minutes since we had stopped, but it felt like an eternity. Mom said, "Bad weather is coming."

I asked her, "How can you tell?"

Mack answered my question, "Stop asking stupid questions, kid, and feel the change in the air." I was insulted and about to tell him off, when I spotted our three humans running back to the trailer. This was strange behavior. Usually they walked back to unload us. It was more common for them to be laughing and joking once they had located our assigned stalls. I was distracted from their bizarre behavior by the sick, greenish color of the sky. I had never seen a green sky! Just before they reached us, great peels of thunder and huge bolts of lightning vibrated through the trailer. I had been through a lot of spring thunderstorms and a few winter snowstorms, it is part of life near the great lakes, but I never felt anything this ominous.

Wind roared in and around us, and I felt my ears pop as the air pressure changed. Katie unhooked the bar across the back of our trailer so Emma could unload Mom.

"Go Emma! We will be right behind you!" Katie yelled into the rising wind.

A bad feeling came over me, and I was beginning to tremble. It did not escape my notice that Patty had come through the front door, and was leading Mack out that way. None of us ever exited through the front door! I felt Katie hook a lead in my halter, disconnect the trailer tie, and place her hand on my chest. I didn't even need that small bit of guidance. I backed down the ramp the way that a racehorse bolts from a starting gate. The wind had gone eerily quiet, and I felt as if someone had sucked all the air out of the world as I scooted out of the trailer. I shook my head attempting to clear my ears. I struggled to breathe in what again seemed like an alien environment.

A heavy wall of black clouds hung just below the strange green skyline. Before I took two steps to follow Mom and Emma, the fierce wind returned, and it had doubled its strength. It was blowing so hard that it rained sideways! Katie and I ran to follow Emma and Mom. Emma had a hold of Mom and was trying to open the overhead door to lead Mom inside. The door was locked! Someone had closed and locked the door just before Emma had gotten there. Katie yelled above the roaring wind, "Emma, follow me!"

Icy rocks fell from the sky and stung me as they bounced off of my back and rump. I was told later that what I had experienced was called hail. I lowered my head, tucked my tail between my legs, and ran along with Katie. Mom and Emma were right behind us, but I was not aware of Patty and Mack. Katie ran to a small door, and she pulled it open. I had seen people go in and out of these small doors, but it looked like a tight fit for a horse. Amazingly, I fit through the small door. I was used to following wherever Katie went, and I responded to the urgency in her voice. "Come, Sox! Hurry boy!"

Emma was right behind us and through the door, when Mom let out a terrified whinny. A loud roaring sound blocked out my mother's voice. Katie dropped my lead rope and made a disparate grab for Emma, and screamed at her to let go of my mother. Several large cowboys restrained Katie, who was determined to go after Emma, and another one closed the door.

I stood rooted to the floor, with my lead rope dangling. I let out a loud whinny, calling to my mother, but she didn't answer me. She was gone, and Emma too! The wind had blown them away, right before my eyes. It had picked them up and carried them away like they were dried up leaves. My heart was heavy in my chest, and every part of me felt sad. I forgot about my small bruised spots from the hail.

Focused on the door where Mom and Emma had vanished, I had not noticed that Patty and Mack had not come inside. It was no wonder that Katie was frantic. Both of our girls were missing, as well as my mom. She calmed down a little when Patty and Mack joined us. They had found another way in.

The monster wind left just as quickly as it had come. When the large overhead door opened again, we walked out into a warm sunny afternoon. I filled my lungs with the clean fresh air, and then I blinked my eyes. I could not believe what I was seeing! Our truck and trailer were gone! All that remained was a silver truck that had been parked next to us, but the trailer that it had been towing was stuck in the middle of a shed row. Behind the main barn, where we had taken shelter, were six shed rows. Each shed row was made up of ten to twelve horse stalls. Horses housed in these stalls could look out of the half doors and still be protected by the overhanging roof. Fortunately, these outside stalls were not in use for this show.

The huge silver trailer was wedged in the center of the second shed row; it had landed on the roof of the barn and fallen through. The first shed row barn was just a pile of sticks, but barns three through six were undamaged. Our green truck and trailer were on their side. They had been flung into the hay field behind the last barn. I was sure glad that we were not in the trailer for that trip. Katie and Patty salvaged our saddles and bridles from the mangled trailer. They saddled Mack and me up, and then we began our search for Mom and Emma.

People continued searching the first two barns. No one had been found, yet. Emma and mom were still missing. The sheriff and local emergency crews were preoccupied rescuing people in a nearby town that had been damaged by the storm. It was up to us to find our missing companions. We found out much later that three tornados had been spotted and touched down in the county.

Additional humans who had arrived early to help with preparations for the weekend show continued to search through the rubble. Mack and I searched with Patty and Katie in one direction. Other horses and their riders went in other directions. Some people went on foot, and some took cars and trucks. Mack said that there might be more people missing than Mom and Emma.

About a quarter of a mile from the show grounds, I thought I heard something. Taking a deep breath, I projected my voice like a country or rock star trying to reach the people at the back of a concert without the aid of a microphone. The sound was faint, but I recognized my mother's voice. I hollered, "Mom, Emma, where are you?"

"Here, Sox. We are here," she called out to me.

Letting my reins hang loose, Katie gave me my head and told me, "Go find them, Sox." Katie knew that I had better hearing than she or

Patty. I picked my way through a muddy field, and I carefully walked around large wood beams scattered over the ground. When my mother's voice got closer, Katie and Patty began to call out to Emma.

Along the way, we found three strange-looking creatures. They stood in the center of the county road and just watched us. Mack said that they were cows. Cows were not part of my learning experience, and I knew nothing about them. However, it occurred to me that they must not be very smart, or they would not keep standing in the middle of the road. It was hard to tell what color they were. The small herd resembled clay or mud sculptures that had magically come to life. They mooed at us in scared pitiful voices.

"The storm moved them, and they are confused," Mack told me.

"What kind of a storm could move those big cows?" I asked him. Mack was new to our horse family, and I thought that he might like to tell tall tales.

"It was probably a twister," he said.

Mack talked funny, real slow, and he used words that I had never heard before. He said "howdy" instead of "hello." He was always saying things like "I reckon," and "y'all."

"What is a twister?" I asked, while we tried to move the muddy cows out of the road.

"Some folks call them tornados. Twisters can move much bigger things than a cow. They can move buildings bigger than our barn. What do you think moved and mangled our horse trailer?" He drawled out his explanation, obviously disgusted with my limited knowledge.

I didn't answer him. Now I knew the name of the roaring monster that broke our trailer, destroyed the outside row of stalls as it parked a trailer on its roof, and then plucked Mom and Emma from our midst. Moving the muddy bovines was frustrating. Impatient with the delay, I called out to my mother again.

She sounded closer, and this time Emma answered my call too, but her voice sounded faint and far away. I left the stupid cows to focus all my attention on locating my mother and Emma. As soon as Mack and I successfully navigated the drainage ditch on the opposite side of the road, we crossed through a tree line that bordered an open field. The muddy herd moved from the road, and they began to follow our trail. Once through the screen of trees, I could see my mother, at least I thought it was my mother. It sounded like Mom, but she was the equine equivalent of the mud cows that were now plodding close behind us.

I stood by my mother's side, while Katie checked on Emma. When we reached them, Emma was sitting in the muddy field. She was still clutching the lead rope, with Mom's empty halter hanging from it. She looked confused, like the pitiful cows that just stood looking around. She too was dazed, and unsure of where she was. Katie had difficulty trying to pry Emma's fingers from the lead rope.

That Friday and the frightening storm that came with it, I will never forget. I hope none of us ever experience it again. I was worried about my little friend. She left in an ambulance and I did not see her for a few days. Katie had called Emma's mother from the barn before we left on our search. She called Hanna again once we found Emma and Mom.

Cell phones are what those little square devices were. Patty used one so much that I thought she had a strange growth on her ear, but I did not know that Katie had one too. The phones were how they got help for Emma, for my mom, and for the muddy cows.

I waited with Mom, Patty, Mack, and three sad cows, while Katie went in the ambulance with Emma.

A short time later, four horse trailers showed up. We walked back to the road, weaving a path through the storm debris. Patty helped load Mack and me into a strange trailer. I was reluctant to get into the trailer.

I had been taught to wait for Katie wherever she had dismounted, and I was going to wait for her. Patty put Mack in first, and then she convinced me to join him. Friends had come from the horse show and brought their horse trailers to help us, but so did horsemen that we had never met before. Mom went in a trailer by herself, and she was taken to a veterinarian. Mack and I rode together back to the show grounds. Our parade of trailers included two that were transporting the mud cows, and they went back with us. Safely back in our stalls, Patty fed us, and we waited for word about our injured companions.

Slim had driven down in the older blue truck, and he pulled us home in our old red trailer. He had dropped off Emma's mom at the hospital and brought Katie back to the show grounds. Surprised and relieved, I saw that Mom was already on board when Mack and I were put in the trailer for the trip home. It smelled like the vet, and I was a little hesitant about entering the old trailer until I realized the odor was coming from my mom. She had ointment on the little scrapes, and her shoulder was bandaged. She wore leg wraps, the same as Mack and I, but her left knee was bandaged above her blue leg wrap.

Bruised and scraped, Emma had also been in shock, but she was not hurt badly. Mom had to have a piece of a splintered board removed from her shoulder, and her right knee had to be stitched as well.

When Mom was feeling better, she told me what happened. She said, "You know how it feels, when Katie uses the horse vacuum on us during the winter? Well, Sox, it was kind of like being sucked up by a giant vacuum cleaner. We felt a terrible pressure in our ears. As we spun around, I knew that Emma was still close, but I couldn't see her. I had my eyes closed to protect them from the stinging mud and other debris that buffeted us. Something sharp hit my shoulder, and then I tumbled to the ground.

Emma was still with me when I hit the ground, but my halter broke and it fell off of my head. I struggled to my feet and looked around for her. My knee hurt, and it was hard to walk.

I found her sitting in the field holding my lead rope with my broken halter still attached. She looked like she was trying to wake up from a bad dream, and she was covered with mud. Twigs, leaves, and mud matted her hair, just like it matted my mane and tail. I put my muzzle on her, and I softly nuzzled her, but she just continued to sit in the grass and stare blankly at our surroundings. It felt like we were in that field forever, and then I heard you call to us. I tried to answer but my voice was weak and shaky. I was so grateful that you heard me, Sox."

"You were not too far away, Mom, but it took us a while to get to you. We had to pick our way through pastures littered with broken fences, downed trees, and the remnants of a barn," I said.

"Was that the cow barn, son?" Mom asked me. "Yes, Mom, I heard that it was the home of the cows that we found in the middle of the road. Do you remember the muddy cows that followed us across the field to you and Emma? I was there when the dairy farmer told Katie that the three cows we found were the only survivors from his small herd. His barn was destroyed too, but his home was spared and his family was unharmed."

Mom said, "I heard Katie tell Slim that we were very lucky to survive our ride in the tornado. She also said that you were a hero. It was your keen hearing, intelligence, and extremely loud voice that led them to us so quickly."

"I am not a hero. I was just looking for those I love. Mack and Patty were with Katie and me. It took all of us to rescue you and Emma, as well as a lot of help to get you out of there."

"You are still my hero, son."

Well, what more could I say? It was OK with me, if Mom thought that I was her hero.

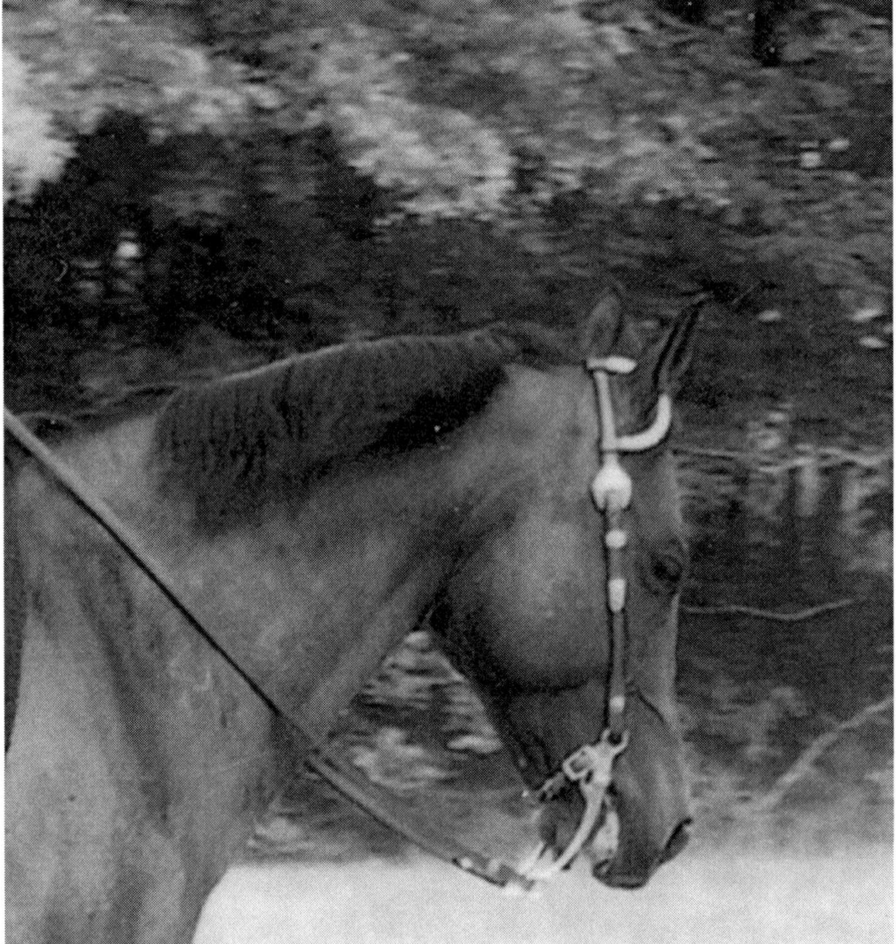

9

BACK IN THE GAME

Our comfortable horse trailer never made it home again after the big storm. Mack and I rode in the old, red, four-horse trailer—he and I in the back two stalls, side by side, and our feed, hay, tack trunk and other junk in the front two stalls. I sure missed the slant stall trailer and the ramp. It had been a long time since I had to hop into a trailer and ride with my head pointed down the highway. I had to adjust my road surfing style, but I knew that we were lucky. We still had Mom and Emma.

I am reluctant to admit it, but Mack was a darn good reining horse. We had been out three weekends in a row, and he had accumulated five wins and was in the money every time he entered the reining pen. Worst of all, he scored seventy-two to seventy-four most of the time.

I hate to be second best, so I put more speed into my large circles and into rundowns before my sliding stops. Still, I only won three times, and twice I didn't place at all. Maybe I tried too hard. I tried to increase the speed on my spins too much, and I was unable to shut down. I overspun and received a score of zero.

I am not making excuses, but it is possible that I was distracted. A guy has to be able to concentrate on the job at hand. It is not that I don't appreciate all the attention, but this hero stuff is starting to get on my nerves. Mothers always think that their sons are heroes, so I just took Mom's praise in stride. However, word had gotten around about the storm rescue, and it had grown with every telling. Curious people were always popping up to pet me or take a photo standing next to me.

"Hero" or "Hollywood," Mack called me and laughed at his own joke. He told me that I was such a celebrity that I should try out for the movies. He said, "Sox, you might be better as a movie horse than a reining horse."

It wasn't until Katie and Patty entered us in the same ladies reining class that Mack stopped teasing me. Patty and Mack went before Katie and me. They scored a seventy-three, and we scored seventy-three and a half. The half point put us in first place, and I got a win over Mack.

Emma had resumed riding by working the Gunner. She regained her strength and seat quickly. My celebrity status had faded by the time that Emma and I entered our first reining class. Katie paired us up right after the fourth of July, and it didn't take us long to develop as a team.

Mom was in foal, her injuries were severe, and she could not show anymore, but the wild ride inside the twister hadn't hurt the foal that she now carried. Slim and Katie decided to retire her; Mom would be a broodmare from now on. In addition to my reining duties, I was now Emma's replacement 4-H horse. Mom might be small in height, but she cast a huge shadow, and I had some awesome hoof prints to fill. So for the first time I went to the fair.

Five years old and well traveled, I thought that I had seen just about everything. Think again! Fair was crazy. I guess the best place to start is with the endless stream of humanity that prowled the aisle ways of the barns. They pushed tiny humans in little covered carts, and some parents carried their little ones in a sling that was strapped to their backs. Then there were the little hoppers. Hoppers were children too small to see over the top of our stalls, so they would jump up to gain enough height to peek in at us. Occasionally, a larger family member would lift them up to get a better look at us horses.

OK, by the second day of the fair I was getting used to the mobs of people at the fair and the fact that they always appeared to be eating. I was enjoying a refreshing bath after a hot afternoon of showing when some of Emma's friends stopped by the wash rack to chat. They were devouring elephant ears! No joke. They were eating ears. I do not know what elephants are, but if they have ears they must be some kind of animal. I had visions of great brown beasts sprinkled with white missing their ears. I thought that the beasts must be huge to have such large ears. I was thankful that my ears were too small to interest these young carnivores.

Showing at the fair is a challenge. Not only do you have to fight your way through the crowds to reach the show ring, you had to dodge other panicked horses too. The first hysterics came during showmanship. We were lined up facing the announcer's stand and ready for the final inspection from the judge. Trotters went racing around the end of the racetrack about one hundred feet behind the show ring. Pounding hooves and rattling sulkies sent several horses in our class up on their hind legs or trying to flee, dragging their young handlers with them. I had seen horse carts before, so I stood my ground. I didn't remember any carts moving so fast, but I didn't think it was very frightening.

The huge draft horse teams and the mammoth wagons they pulled also caused frenzy among the less experienced 4-H mounts. I have to admit to you that the hot air balloon, with its whooshing sound as it barely cleared the announcer's stand, gave me butterflies in my tummy. Many of my fellow 4-H projects got so upset that parents and group leaders came in to assist the young riders.

My first fair had been an education. When I told my mom about my experiences, she just laughed and said, "That sounds about right. If you handled the fair for a full week, son, you can handle almost anything."

Emma and I only showed a couple of more times in August before school started. Mack and I went to a couple of more shows in September. In October, Slim and Katie came home from the All-American Quarter Horse Congress in Columbus with a new truck and a new horse trailer. Both were silver, and memories came back to me of the silver trailer in the middle of the collapsed barn.

Mom had been to the Quarter Horse Congress when she was young, and I wondered when I would get a turn. Mom said that it is the largest single breed horse show in the world, and it goes on for three weeks in October at the Ohio State Fairgrounds. We spent October and November riding the trails the same as always. I was blanketed by the end of August, and when I went out to play I wore a turnout blanket. Then I left home on the first of December. I was prepared to spend another winter at the boarding stable, and it looked like Mack was going to accompany me.

My first clue that something was different was when I heard Buddy's excited bark. It was the same sound that he made when Katie let him travel to the shows with the rest of us. The second clue came when Slim turned the wrong way out of the drive. Our winter boarding stable was in the other direction.

Most of my travels had been confined to Ohio and neighboring states. This time I traveled all the way across the Ohio River, through Kentucky and Tennessee, with their steep roads that wound through mountains. It was such a relief to hit the long flat stretch of road through Georgia and into Florida.

We spent our first night with some horse friends in Tennessee. When we got into the trailer the next morning, we no longer had our blankets on. By the time we stopped for the second night, we were traveling with our windows down. Everything was different in Florida!

It had been snowing when we left home, and here it was like summer. Fresh cool breezes from the great lakes were replaced by soft, warm winds from the ocean that sometimes lifted our damp manes. From our temporary home we could smell oranges. I was later told that what I had smelled were really the orange blossoms. Florida had some strange-looking trees that Katie called palms. People here decorated them with Christmas lights, just like our humans did to the pine trees in Ohio.

We got our usual stocking with dried apples, carrots, and peppermints. The Christmas stocking was a big comfort to me. I was a bit homesick. Mack had never had a Christmas stocking before, and that surprised me.

I thought that all horses got Christmas stockings! During our time in Florida, we also got to give rides to Bill's little children. They were so small that another rider had to hold them in their lap.

Katie and Patty worked us harder now that we were more used to the climate change. We worked early in the morning before the heat of the day. Reining shows in Florida begin in January, and we were ready for them. Some of the shows were outdoors, but the bigger shows were in covered arenas. I have been working and showing in indoor arenas since I was two, but our arenas at home have walls all the way to the roof. Some are even heated.

The arenas here looked like a roof on poles; the sides were open, and it allowed the air through while it kept the hot sun out. There were fans above us to help circulate the air. The ground was good, and we brought home a few paychecks and a couple of trophy plaques. We showed in January and part of February, while Slim, Katie, and Patty visited Bill and his new family.

Patty left before the rest of us. She flew to New York for a meeting. I knew that Patty was smart and talented, but I did not know that she could fly too!

On the return trip, we got our blankets put on before we got to Tennessee. Mack and I didn't go home; we were dropped off at the boarding stable where I had spent the previous four winters.

Katie started riding Mack too. Three days a week she would ride Mack, while Emma rode me. I was happy. I was home, and I was working with Emma once more.

We stayed home through March and practiced our timing. Somewhere in the middle of that month, Emma told me that I had a little brother. I did not meet him until the beginning of June, when Mack and I went home for the summer. He was the same color as Mom and he too didn't have one white marking. Our humans called him Doc, or Little Doc, or Doc E Doodle. What they called him depended on how cute that they thought he was at the time. The fuss they made over him was downright disgusting. It was hard for me to believe that I was ever that little, or that cute.

Mom's unease about bad weather does not bother Little Doc. He is so calm, and I think that he reassures Mom. Nightmares still haunted my mother whenever the weather turned bad. The tornado had left scars on her, and she had a slight limp.

Emma too had become very nervous during threatening weather and tension radiated from her as she scanned the sky for frightening dark clouds. Hanna, Katie, and I took turns reassuring her.

Mack, Handy, and I were the exiled bachelors. We occupied a different pasture than the mares and my little brother. At times I would catch him looking at us the way I used to look at the other horses when I was little and Mom and I were kept separated from them.

As a six-year-old our schedule changed, and we traveled east more often. We went further into Pennsylvania. New York was included our travels because Patty worked and lived there. She was able to drive to the shows in the East. Competition was tough in our reining classes, but we held our own.

Mack was collecting a lot of big paychecks along with an increasing collection of pewter trophies that looked like a reining horse and rider. He now had three bronze trophies that also looked like a reining horse and rider.

Emma and I were doing great in the youth fourteen to eighteen age group, and we were always in the top three in the rookie reining class.

On occasion, Mack and I would end up competing in the same class, when Katie and Patty rode us in the ladies reining or the jackpot gelding class. A challenge was issued by Patty—the rider with the lowest score had to buy dinner. I think that the results were sort of even on the dinner bet. Mack and I usually scored close, and I scored above him as much as he outscored me. We even tied a couple of times, and once we had a run off for first place.

On our first run we scored seventy-four. Katie and I went first on the tiebreaking run. She rode me at an easy pace, and we aimed at a correct and penalty-free pattern. I completed my second run with a score of only seventy and a half. Patty and Mack were having a good run, and it looked like Katie was going to buy dinner. We were running pattern two, and the spins were the final maneuver. Mack spun to the right so fast that he was a blur, and he spun equally fast to the left, but instead of the required four spins he did five. Patty got so excited by Mack's awesome second effort that she lost count of the rotations on the last set of spins. She called it pilot error.

On the 4-H end of things, Emma and I qualified to represent our county at the state fair. Emma wanted to take me to the Quarter Horse Congress this year. She had been saving up for a long time to go to Columbus for the Congress, and she gave up our spot to go there for the Ohio State Fair. So we stayed home and went to our county fair, while the alternate 4-H horse and rider went to state.

Our workouts changed following fair. Emma carried her guitar when she cooled me out after our workouts. I loved music, and I loved when Emma played her guitar, but I was not crazy about her playing it on my back. We made several trips a week to our winter boarding stable to practice in the large indoor arena. I had some trouble with the guitar bumping me, and I had to get used to it.

In September in New York, all the practice with the guitar and the music made sense. I entered the show pen, with glitter painted on my rump that looked like notes of music and gold ribbons woven through my mane and tale. Emma glittered too in a white shirt decorated with rhinestones.

Our approach to center arena was at the same relaxed walk as usual, but when we stopped I made a quick quarter turn to the left and stood staring at the judge. Emma started to play her guitar, and I was expecting the recorded music signaling the beginning of our routine. I thought that I was prepared, but the music was not soft like it had been at practice. The music and lyrics boomed out of huge speakers and filled the air. It echoed off the ceiling and bounced off the walls. Emma rolled the guitar around to her back, and we took off to the beat of "Hillbilly Rockstar." True to the lyrics of the song I was off and running, a bit out of control, but the crowd loved us. I outran the music on our first freestyle, so Emma added a few more rotations to my spins and backed me longer to fill up some time. We finished up with another backup after a long sliding stop, and I quit backing to the last note of the song. WOW! My ears were still ringing with the loud music and the noise of the crowd. We placed fifth in the non-pro freestyle, and we found out what needed to be smoothened out before we tried this at the Quarter Horse Congress. Maybe I could put in a request for earplugs.

Freestyle reining is like dancing or figure skating, and keeping time with the music makes a much better impression. Like dancing or skating, it takes a lot of practice to get it right. I got all my required moves in: I had four spins each way, three stops, and a lead change on both directions. My awesome rollbacks and speedy backups were additional maneuvers in freestyle. Horses are allowed a lot of extra maneuvers, but if their routine does not include those required, they will receive a score of zero.

Emma and I made our first trip to the Quarter Horse Congress that year, and we had improved our freestyle routine enough to place third. Awesome and fun! We loved dancing to the music and had become a fantastic team. The Congress was held at the state fairgrounds, and I think that our county fairgrounds felt a lot more comfortable. Our stalls were not close to the show arenas, and we had to walk a long way through thick crowds to get there or to reach the warm-up areas.

Mack was right at home visiting with the horses from Texas stalled near us. They all had a drawl like Mack and talked kind of slow. We were a little nervous in our first few classes. I could feel Emma's knees shaking, and it worried me, but we settled in before our freestyle. Emma and I returned to the Congress the next two years. We also entered every freestyle class that we could find on our show circuit. Emma and Sox: dance team extraordinaire!

10

STEPPING INTO A NEW ROLE

Reining is in my blood. It is hard for me to remember that I struggled with the maneuvers as a young horse. Ten years old now. I love to run, slide, and roll back just horsing around. Backyard horses, we do not have a lot of room to run, but I have learned to maximize my paddock space. Running full out, I tuck my hip under me and circle the paddock like a blur.

My little brother has grown into an amazing reining horse. Call it sibling rivalry. Call it horseplay, or call it showing off. Doc and I have developed a unique pasture game. It began as a simple race between competitive brothers. Just bucking, kicking, and shaking our heads, we were quickly closing in on the fence near the road. Handy and Mack blocked our forward progress. We could not turn without mowing them down. They were ignoring us and concentrating on their conversation, as they obliviously cropped grass. It is hard to say which one of them could tell the biggest whopper. Almost to the fence, as one Doc and I slid to a stop. In unison we rolled back and ran hard in the opposite direction. The game was born!

Part of our game is to try to outrun the other, but we are pretty evenly matched. I miss our game and Doc too, when he goes out to the boarding stable for the winter months. An accomplished reining horse, I am able to spend my winters at home.

A new chapter has begun on my journey, and my life has turned another page. Mom has foaled another colt and a filly, which means I now have two brothers and a sister. My siblings prance alongside me, while I help pony them. Katie and I teach them manners and to travel with another horse the way that my mother had helped to teach me.

Instruction and show and tell have become part of my new role in life. I teach the lessons of a horse's life to the young horses. I travel to 4-H clinics and show the young riders how to perform reining maneuvers. At home, I introduce reining to Katie's more advanced students. I also carry around Slim and Katie's grandchildren when they visit us. Their grandson is the oldest and has longer legs, and it is easier for him to guide me.

Little E. is younger, and she has trouble reaching my sides, but she loves me. She talks to me like Emma used to. Drawing from years of experience, I listen for the familiar commands to walk, trot, or whoa that reach my ears from her small child's voice. I pay extra attention to the little leg bumps on my saddle, because she can't reach my sides yet. Katie's granddaughter is a natural, like Patty and Emma, and it won't be long before she wants to go faster than a walk and trot.

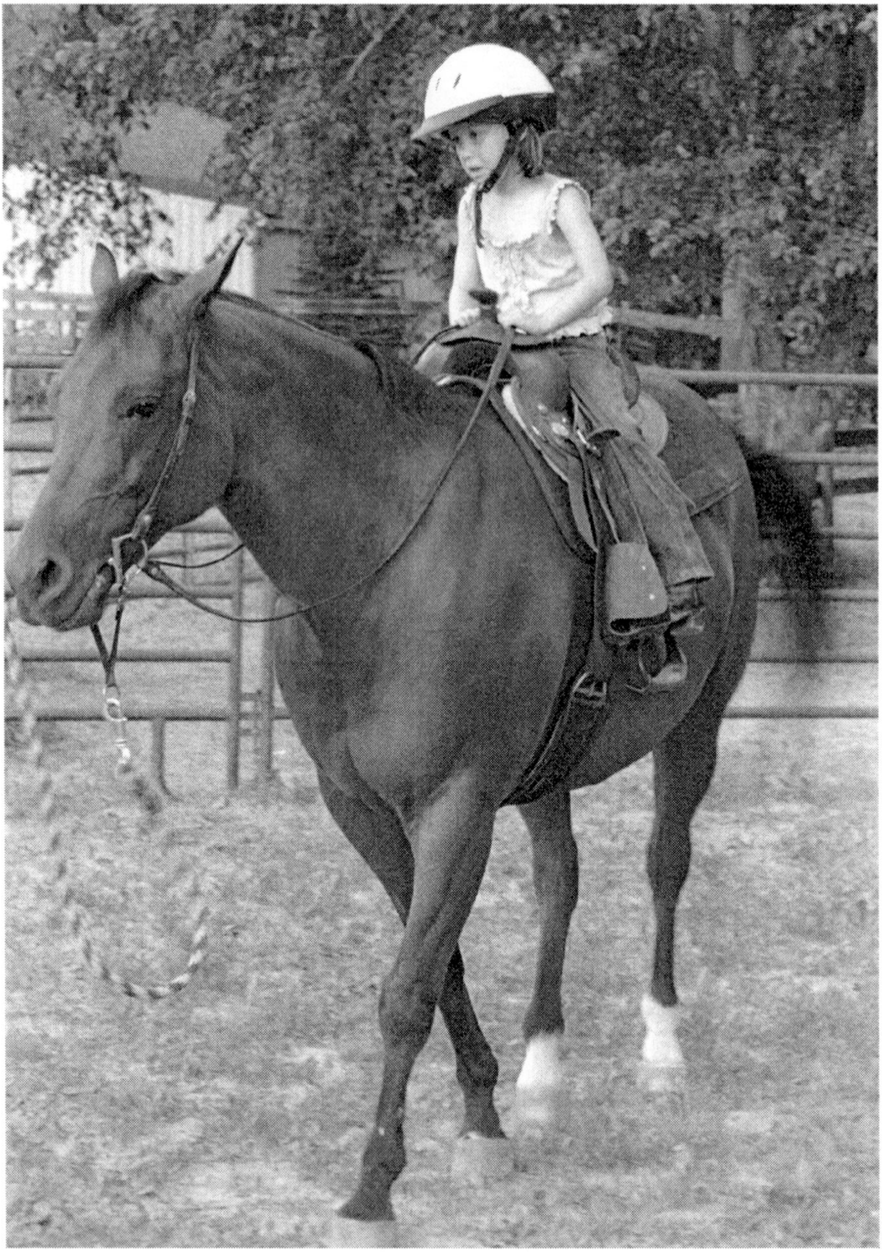

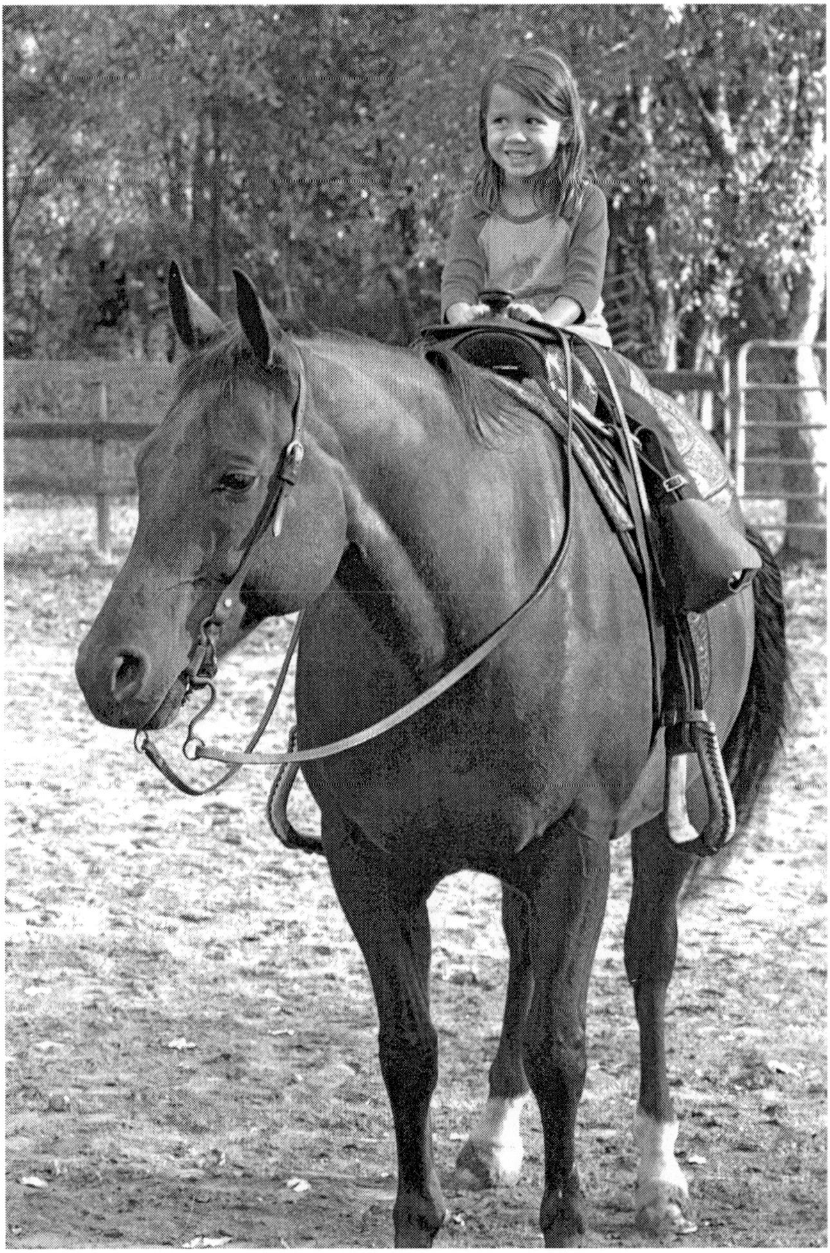

Trail riding in the snow is a new experience that I really enjoy. My slide plates come off for the winter, and when I am not on a trail ride I relax at home. Again I can play in the snow and listen to guitar music coming from Emma's house. Hanna makes the music that drifts into the barn now.

Emma has gone away to college, so I don't see her much anymore. We are still best friends, and she always visits me when she comes home. She made something called the dean's list her first semester at The Ohio State University. She told me that the university was not far from the state fairgrounds in Columbus where we had shown so many times.

On her Christmas break, she brings carrots and apples to supplement the treats in our stockings. Our ears can pick up the joyful sounds of Christmas carols. Two guitars and a piano accompany Emma, her mother, and her grandmother, as they sing. It is a real treat for us.

I look forward to spring break and the summer months that bring Emma back to me. We ride the trails, go to a couple of small local shows, and sometimes we dance to music just for fun.

APPENDIX

PARTS OF A HORSE

1. Muzzle	9. Neck	17. Point of Buttocks	25. Cannon bone
2. Nostril	10. Throatlatch	18. Stifle	26. Knee
3. Cheek	11. Withers	19. Flank	27. Forearm
4. Face	12. Back	20. Gaskin	28. Shoulder
5. Eye	13. Loin	21. Hock	29. Sock
6. Forelock	14. Croup	22. Hoof or Foot	30. Stocking
7. Ear	15. Hip	23. Pastern	
8. Mane	16. Tail	24. Fetlock	

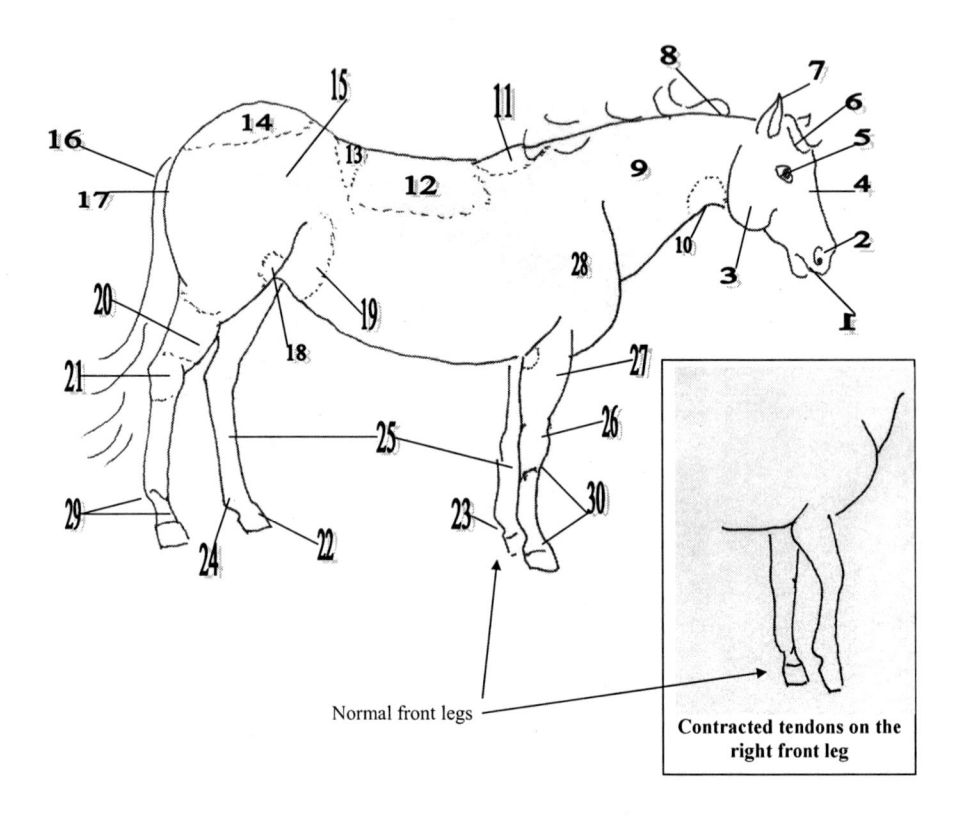

Normal front legs

Contracted tendons on the right front leg

VOCABULARY

Bay—A brown horse, with black main tail and black points. Points are the tips of the ears, the muzzle and black legs from the knees and hocks down.

Biped—An animal, for example, a human, with only two legs for locomotion

Bran-mash—Bran is the outer covering of cereal grains that are partly or completely removed during the milling process. It is a good source of dietary fiber. Adding warm water to the bran makes bran-mash, it is usually wheat bran, and it looks much like oatmeal.

Colt—A male horse under four years of age

Contracted tendons—Flexor tendons and some ligaments are too short, and can make it difficult for the foal to pass through the birth canal. Severe cases may require surgery and a leg cast.

Draft horse—There are many breeds of draft horses. The most famous are the Budweiser Clydesdales. Many small farms, as well as the Amish, use draft horses to work their fields.

Filly—A female horse under four years of age

Foal—A baby horse or pony

Gelding—A male horse that has been neutered

Green horse—A horse with very little experience, usually in the early stages of training

Hand—A hand is four inches. It is the measurement for a horse, taken from the ground to the point of the withers. Example: A fifteen-and horse would be equal to 60", 15.2 hands = 62".

Long-line or Lunge-line—Is a long lead, fifteen to twenty feet long, with a snap at one end

Mare—A female horse four years of age or older

Pony horse—A horse that is used to lead another horse. Racehorses often have a pony horse walk them to the starting gate.

Sibling—A brother or sister (same mother and/or father)

Stallion—A male horse four years of age or older that is usually kept for breeding.

Suckling—A young animal that is still feeding on its mother's milk

Warmblood horses—Are popular with dressage riders and cross-country riders. They are tall horses, seventeen hands to nineteen hands. Most of the breeds were originally imported from Europe. They combine the cold blood of the draft horse with a hot-blooded horse like a thoroughbred.

Weanling—A young horse that has just been taken off of its mother's milk

Yearling—An animal that is between one and two years old. Examples: A horse, a calf, or a deer

MORE ABOUT THE SPORT OF REINING

HISTORY: Reining began as a form of recreation among working cowboys. Cowboys covered many miles on the back of their cowponies gathering and moving herds of cattle. These cowponies had to be quick, agile, and strong. These stock horses were prized for the ability to cover a short distance at a dead run to stop quickly and to change direction in an instant when chasing a stray steer or calf.

Cowponies were adept at neck reining, because the cowboy needed one hand free for his rope or rifle, or even to haze a reluctant steer with his hat or sombrero. Competitions developed between individual cowboys, and often between ranches to determine the horse with the best skills.

Around 1949, the American Quarter Horse Association recognized reining as a sport. In 1966 the National Reining Horse Association was formed in Ohio and remained there until 1997, when it moved to Oklahoma.

Quarter Horses dominate the sport, mostly because working ranchers originally bred them. Many other breed associations have also added reining as a recognized class, but the National Reining Horse Association competitions are open to all breeds.

Reining has spread like a wildfire in the last two decades and the American Quarter Horse has taken up residence in many countries. Over thirty countries around the world have reining associations and hold reining competitions. Since its opening international debut in

Gladstone, New Jersey in June of 2000, reining has earned many new fans. The sport also gained recognition in 2000 from the (FEI) International Federation for Equestrian Sports.

One of the fastest growing horse sports in the world, reining was added to the World Equestrian Games in 2002 at the Games in Jerez, Spain. The 2010 Games were hosted at the Kentucky Horse Park in Lexington, Kentucky. For the first time in its history, reining was showcased on national television as part of the coverage of the World Equestrian Games.

The top individual riders competed in front of millions of viewers for the individual gold, silver, and bronze medals.

Reining competitions can be found at: grassroots shows, 4-H county and state shows, sanctioned NRHA Affiliate circuit shows, and non-NRHA affiliated clubs that sponsor jackpot reinings.

This wide verity of venues offers beginners and casual reiners the opportunity to compete at their skill level and at an economic comfort level.

If you would like to know more about the sport of reining or see some reining videos, try www.nrha.com. You can also learn more about the American Quarter Horse at www.aqha.com. Check out the Foundation Quarter Horse Association at www.fqha.com.

ABOUT THE AUTHOR

Accomplished as an equestrian, with a lifetime of experience as trainer, exhibitor, 4-H and youth club coach, as well as horse show judge, the author brings many years of experience with young riders to her "Backyard Horse Tales."

As a child, **Jackie Anton** chose to play the role of a wild horse when her siblings and friends chose cowboys or Indians. Her love of horses grew, as did her empathy for the horse. These traits developed a unique insight into the equine mind.

A mother and grandmother of two, Jackie continues to ride daily. She lives on a mini-farm in rural Ohio. She shares her little slice of horse heaven with her husband, two Quarter Horses, a thirty-three-year-old Appaloosa, a big fuzzy dog, and a barn cat.

ILLUSTRATOR

Jackie Anton began drawing horses when she was ten. She grew up in the inner city, and the only horses that she had access to were on the TV or the mounts of the Cleveland Police Department. She went to school with the ends from carrots in her pocket for the local beat horse. She drew the police horses and the horses in her mind.

At age fourteen, she got her first job as a stable hand; after school and on weekends she cleaned tack, stalls, and horses. Part of her pay was the access to ride at the end of the workday. Jackie had plenty of models at the riding stable, and she drew them all.

BACKYARD HORSE TALES

FROSTY

FROSTY BRITCHES, an Appaloosa struggling to understand reoccurring visions.

What are the reasons for these strange experiences? Are they only bad dreams, or are they memories of a long ago past? Has Frosty been here before? Was he there with his ancestors, as they fled for their lives, or are his disturbing recollections only stories handed down through the ages?

Turn the page for a sneak preview of the next Backyard Horse Tale.

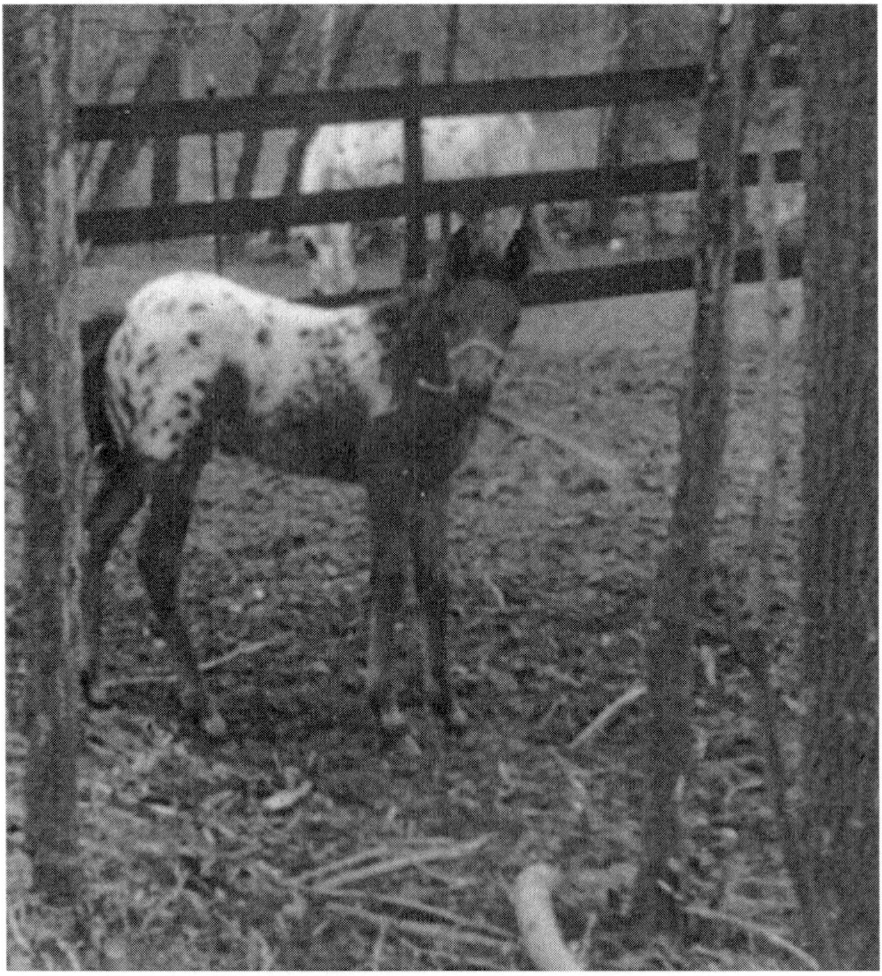

1

OCTOBER 1970, OLMSTED FALLS

Our manes tossed in the cool fall breeze while we waited for the endless procession of train cars. Boxes on wheels, and loaded flat beds with lumber or coils of steel clanked and rumbled past us.

Strong vibrations started in the soles of my feet and traveled up my legs; my heart began to pound like a war drum. My young rider stroked my neck and held me well back from the metal monster.

Joey, my companion, was only three years old, and he was very frightened. I was only a year older than him, but he looked to me for guidance. He too was an Appaloosa.

"Frosty, aren't you scared?" He asked.

I could not lie to him and tell him that I was not afraid. I chose my words carefully, and asked him.

"Joey, are we not the descendants of the great war horses of the Nez Perce?"

My tactic worked. Joey perked his ears, puffed out his chest, and he turned to face the terrifying train. The kid stood his ground, and he made a brave attempt to look as stoic as he thought I was.

Once the train passed, we watched as a parade of cars and trucks bounced over the tracks from both directions. Our riders held us back until there was a break in the traffic. Finally moving forward, we stepped from the side of the paved road onto the train tracks. The ground tremor was fading, but I could still feel the train as I stepped onto the tracks.

Joey regained his confidence and settled down quickly once we entered the park. A warm afternoon sun filtered through the canopy of brightly colored trees, and the rain of leaves formed a layer over the bridle path. We followed the multicolored ribbon winding among the tree-covered hills. Bright red, orange, gold, and many shades of brown leaves made a pleasant crunching sound beneath our hooves as we walked along.

Joey and I only occasionally tossed our heads, or flicked our tails at a fly. The cool fall air kept many of the flies away, and they did not annoy us as much as they had during the summer. We jogged and loped along, following a trail that resembled a multicolored ribbon winding its way through the trees.

Muscles twitched beneath my skin, and it did not have anything to do with dislodging another fly. I tried to focus on the trail, but my skin felt prickly the way that it always did before one of my visions. Marcie stroked my neck, and her voice brought me back from the edge before I could slip into that other world. Marcie and I have been together three years, and sometimes we were able to read the other one's thoughts. It has always been like that . . .

* * *

Happy and carefree, I romped with the other colts on the farm where I was born. I was not upset at weaning time, unlike some of the other weanlings. My mother had prepared me for weaning; she also told me that she was carrying another foal, and that it was time for me join the rest of the herd. Early the following spring, I was able to see my little sister run and play before I left the farm.

Marcie had come to look at an older horse, but we were meant to be together. I followed her around as she rode the Palomino mare outside the fenced pasture that enclosed me and the rest of the herd. She watched me as I tracked them. The truth is she could not keep her eyes off of me. I know how that sounds, and believe me I am not vain. I know that there are many pretty horses, some are much prettier than me, but there was this instant connection between us.

So two months into my yearling spring, I went home with Marcie. The first two years of my life were mostly uneventful. Marcie and I went to a few horse shows, where she showed me at halter. I guess that the judges liked me because I always got a ribbon, but most of the time I came in second place, or maybe third. Marcie said that many of the judges liked to place loud color when they judged the yearling stallions.

Maybe Marcie was right; most of the winners that got their ribbons before I received mine were leopard horses, or horses with huge blankets loaded with spots. I was a dark chocolate color then, with black spots under my dark coat and just a little sprinkle of white hairs on my rump that looked a bit like sugar. A star decorated the middle of my forehead, and I wore one white sock on my left hind foot. Like most of the foundation Appaloosas of my time, I had pink skin with dark spots that really showed up around my eyes and nose. My hooves were striped, and the white ringed my brown eyes. These traits are attributed to my kind of horse.

* * *

The spring I turned two was when my strange visions began. It was at this time that I became a gelding. The vet gave me a shot to put me to sleep. My head felt heavy, and everything became fuzzy. I braced my legs so that I would not fall over, but he gave me another shot, and I sank to my knees in the front paddock, and I rolled over on to my side.

I woke up stretched out in the sun, but I was no longer in the front paddock of the boarding stable in Ohio. I didn't know where I was. I tried to stand, but my legs were shaky like the legs of a newborn foal. At first I thought that my confusion and weak legs were a result of the double whammy of shots that had put me to sleep. After I gained my feet, I struggled to focus my eyes. Panic started to overtake me.

Standing on a hill overlooking a crystal clear river, I blink to clear my vision. On the opposite bank graze hundreds of horses; most of them are easily recognizable as Appaloosas. Behind the grazing herd, I see snowcapped mountains. Had the vet given me too much tranquilizer? Am I dead and is this horse heaven? I am frightened, and I want to go back to Marcie, but I don't know how to get there.